Queen of the Fae

Book Two in the Fae Unbound Series

Jill Nojack

IndieHeart Press
Kent, Ohio

Cover designed by Lou Harper.

Visit the series website for series related content:

www.faeunbound.com

Queen of the Fae / Jill Nojack. — 1st ed.

ISBN: 978-0-9911234-1-4

CHAPTER ONE
Don't Bother Me

TANJI POURED ANOTHER GLASS of iced tea and offered some to Lizbet across the picnic table. "Did I tell you my dad's new business is taking off? I guess a lot of people are upset about their gardens being overrun with gnomes, and 'Ron Ross's Humane Gnome Removal and Magical Pest Control' is a good idea." Tanji grinned as she drew broad air quotes around the name, "He's building this giant garden out by my granddad's old fishing cabin. And he put this hu-u-uge ceramic gnome in the middle. It even has little gnome-size houses in the garden and everything. I think he's going to try to civilize them."

"Good luck with that!" Lizbet said, "Gnomes are *gross*. I mean capital-G gross. Even my mom tried to remove her ceramic gnomes from the back garden, and you know how committed she was to them before Fae Day. She hoped the real ones would leave if she did. But the gnomes have them fastened down somehow. She can't budge them."

Lizbet cocked her head toward the end of the garden where her little brother was joyfully running after a group of gnomes. "Of course, Bobby thinks the gnomes are uber-cool. He's an eight year old boy. He wants to marry anything that farts and burps every couple of minutes." Lizbet rubbed her temples. "Me? Not so much. Their squealing just makes my head hurt."

"Your head always hurts. It's been a month since Fae Day. You should feel better by now—I know you don't want to believe it, but I think there's more going on inside your brain than you think there is. Like, something *fae* that isn't right."

"You're making too big a deal out of it," Lizbet said as she gave Tanji a half-smile. "My doctor says I should do yoga or something because the headaches are probably just stress from all of the attention. I mean, let's face it—the press and bloggers only stopped camping out outside of the house like a week ago. And I'm still getting email and messages every day from haters who blame me because they don't want to have the fae around. You know—plus I got hit by lightning. Big, crashy lightning."

"Look, if everything's normal, then why don't you have Morgan's memories and magic like I've got Langoureth's? Why do you only have the wings and a giganto headache?"

"Can't you just leave it alone? Because I don't know—maybe because I had the human side of Morgan in there already? I don't want the wings, I don't want the magic, and I definitely don't want a bunch of fae forcing me to take Morgan's place as queen, so I'm glad I don't have her memories. Maybe I don't have Morgan's memories or magic because I just don't want them." Lizbet grimaced. "How about we just have a conversation as Tanji and Lizbet and not so much as chicks with past lives?"

Tanji flounced off with the pitcher to make more iced tea. "Sure, whatever. It's your head, not mine."

Lizbet drifted away into her own thoughts: she'd changed the world forever when she freed the fae from the shadow realm, and a lot of people weren't happy about it. It was difficult for people to adjust to having magic and fairies hanging around doing magical-fairy things when the fae hadn't been around for over a millennium.

She knew she wouldn't do anything differently if Eamon showed up in her garden asking for her help again, but she felt like she owed a lot of people for the negatives of having the fae around—especially the half-fae like Tanji who didn't sign up for suddenly having their lives completely blown off course. She owed her boyfriend James even more for being a part of forcing the memories of a long-dead wizard into his brain.

She must have drifted too long because Tanji brought her back to reality just as her wings started flapping around for no reason for the third or fourth time since they'd parked themselves on the porch. "So, you still here, or am I hanging out with myself?"

"Yep, me and my annoying big ol' fairy wings are still here," Lizbet replied.

Tanji looked over admiringly at the colorful, bright blue, iridescent wings. "Girl, I get that you have no interest in being famous or being a queen, but the wings? The wings are fierce. You should keep the wings."

~~*

Bobby called out, "Ready or not, here I come," and uncovered his eyes. He moved quickly around the back garden, trying to spot the hidden gnomes and tag them before they could get back to the tree that served as home base, or, as they often did when they were cheating, disappear down a burrow hole.

Gurrdenn, the huddle's chief, darted out from under a fern and ran behind Bobby, heading swiftly for the home tree. Bobby trailed after him and tripped, landing on his hands and knees. He had no time to recover. Four gnomes crawled quickly onto his back, trying to knock each other off. Hide and seek had turned into king of the mountain, and the gnomes who made it to the top started shrieking, "Won, won, won."

Bobby wished they could get the rules straight just once, but they never did. Plus, they almost always forgot what they were playing and ran off to investigate a glimmer of light through the trees or an interesting sound. They were fun to play with sometimes, but it wasn't that much fun when they suddenly ran off toward the woods in the middle of a game shouting, "Shiny, shiny, shiny!"

"Gurrdenn, we're playing hide and seek, not king of the mountain! You guys didn't win. I won. I used my back to tag all of you."

As Bobby got up, the gnomes slid down his back, still chanting, "Won, won, won."

"Lost, lost, lost!" shouted Bobby loudly, the effort reddening his face to a shade that nearly matched his unkempt, curly red hair.

Gurrdenn ran in a circle around Bobby's legs, still chanting, and punctuating every rendition of the word "won" with a loud burp. The other gnomes followed suit. Bobby couldn't help but laugh. Soon, he was jumping, laughing, and chanting with them and feeling the tiniest bit left out because he couldn't manage to burp on cue.

He'd rather have his mom, dad, and sister pay attention to him, but Lizzie always had a headache, and his parents paid way more attention to her since she came home from Scotland. His father stopped by a lot now, but it was to check on his sister, mostly about whether or not she had managed to "get rid of the wings yet". From the way his daddy said it, he didn't think daddy liked the wings much. Bobby didn't think the wings were all that special, either. They were pretty, but Lizbet couldn't even fly, so why have them? Everybody always made a big deal about her wings one way or the other except for the gnomes. They stayed far away from her.

The very best thing he liked about the gnomes was they didn't want anything to do with his sister. They only liked Bobby, and Bobby thought that was just fine.

"Dad's talked about having me open a store for real magic—potions or spell ingredients...only the non-dangerous stuff—for people who want to try their hand with it now that it exists. He's like, cranked up to make it a family business. I think it would be a cool way to get some work experience before college, but I don't know if I have enough time."

"Sure you do, you know you do. You can go to school, do your homework, date, and run a retail empire. No problem. You're the Tanjinator. Nothin' you can't do, right?" The girls laughed. "Your father should add pixies and ghouls to his list of fae pests. I know I wouldn't want a ghoul hanging around my loved ones right after they were buried. Nobody wants to find out Aunt Gertie got eaten."

"Eww, really?"

"Yep. According to Eamon, ghouls are real. Your dad should ask him about it."

Both of the girls looked out to the back garden when Bobby shrieked, and they laughed when they saw him on his knees, covered with gnomes. Tanji poked her friend's arm, "You have to admit, the little guys are kind of cute from a distance. Bobby always seems to have fun with them."

"Dad's talking about getting him a dog, but Mom says Dad doesn't live here anymore, and *she's* not going to be the one who ends up taking care of it. But he just keeps saying, 'a really big dog.' He thinks the gnomes might move on if he sticks a dog in the yard, but I'm thinking they'd just eat it."

"Whoa girl, that's grim."

"Just being realistic. Do you know how awful my mom felt when she had to return the neighbor cat's collar and explain what happened? Bobby says that he told the gnomes they aren't allowed to eat any cats or dogs and to definitely not make any clothes out of the cat's fur, but I don't think they'll listen. Really, what's the point of gnomes?"

"To make more gnomes?"

"Exactly." Lizbet glared down the garden at the gnomes as their high, piercing voices grew louder while they chanted. Their shrill calls were so annoying—every time she heard them, it aggravated the pain in her head.

Lizbet's voice hardened in a way Tanji had never heard her speak before. "I cannot stand gnomes." She stood up and walked rapidly to where Bobby and the gnomes were playing. They were so engaged in their dance they didn't see her coming.

Lizbet seized a gnome roughly in each hand and then pulled them up in the air, each of them dangling by one leg. "I cannot stand gnomes."

Tanji watched, shocked, as the other gnomes ran off and scrambled into their burrow, squealing in gnomish, "Hide, hide, the queen, the queen!" The part of her that was a fifteen hundred year old fae understood what the gnomes said, and she didn't like what she heard. It wasn't Lizbet out there. It was Lizbet's fae side, Morgan.

Lizbet/Morgan was raging around the garden now, calling out threats to the gnomes whose heads popped out of burrow holes and then vanished again as quickly as they'd appeared.

She swung the terrified gnomes back and forth as she stomped. Then she pulled one arm back, preparing to swing the head of the unfortunate gnome against the trunk of a nearby tree, when Bobby ran in front of her, his freckles standing out against a face drained of color by fear. He yelled "Lizzie, don't! What are you doing? You don't hurt people! Please, Lizzie. Please, don't!"

Lizbet's expression changed suddenly from fury to blankness. Then she looked at the gnomes in each of her hands and gently set them down on the ground. The other gnomes began to come cautiously back out of the burrow. Lizbet continued to stand there silently, looking unsure about what had just happened. The gnomes whispered to each other, "Just the girl now, just the girl."

Gurrdenn tugged on Bobby's pant leg, and when Bobby looked down, Gurrdenn winked, "Won the queen. Bobby won the queen."

Bobby didn't understand the gnomish word for queen that Gurrdenn used instead of the simple English the gnomes were learning, but Tanji did. She bustled Lizbet toward the porch as the gnomes began to dance around Bobby again, chanting, "Won the queen, won the queen, won the queen."

"What just happened there, Lizzie?" Tanji asked.

"I don't know."

"That's the problem. You never do. But I think Morgan finally made her intentions known," Tanji said, laying a hand gently on her friend's shoulder.

CHAPTER TWO

Close To You

JAMES TEXTED, "HAVE THE wisps been following u 2?"

In a few minutes, he got Lizbet's reply "no, they ignore me"

"i thnk they feel myrddin in here and know he is mssing his fae hlf"

There was no reply. After several minutes, he tapped out, "Bad tme?"

"hdache i m napping"

"i worry abt u. skype l8er?"

"if i cn first day of school tmorrw"

James shoved his phone into his back pocket and looked back to the spiral notebook where he'd been recording Myrddin's spell knowledge as it surfaced. Most of what he was willing to write down for Thomas would have been really helpful in a time when there weren't hospitals, doctors, or safe living conditions.

Myrddin had been a man of peace, and James was glad of that. Even though he didn't like having memories that didn't belong to him, he could at least live with the kind of man Myrddin had been. He couldn't imagine what Lizbet must go through dealing with memories of the eight other lives that had been thrust on her when Eamon slapped Morgan le Fae's amulet around her neck. She hadn't had a choice any more than he had.

Thomas called to James from the small kitchen where he was mixing herbs and cooking up his latest potions. "All right then, James?"

"Yeah, I guess. Lizbet's still having headaches, so I worry about that. And she's still stuck with the wings."

"She'd embrace them if she fully understood the honor it is to be even partially fae."

James rolled his eyes. He'd grown to like Thomas and appreciate his sober—and often entertaining—approach to the world. It was more suited to an eighty year old than a twenty-one year old. But Thomas seemed destined to be a zealot in every lifetime. Although he no longer had the memories of a long-dead Roman monk, he was as single-minded in his devotion to the fae as the monk Faolan had been to the Roman church. It worried James, but he hadn't seen Thomas doing anything that seemed dangerous to other people since they'd come to London, so his obsession was probably harmless. Still, Thomas's interest in traveling to one of the elves' fortresses to get to know his magical counterparts would be a very bad idea.

Thomas was convinced the elves would accept him as one of their own if he became a powerful enough sorcerer, but Thomas was only one-fourth fae and one-eighth elf, and neither was by birth. His magic was the result of the remerge of what the fae called a wisp which had been created when Faolan split the realms. They consisted of the magic that had been pulled from the bodies of humans who were less than half fae but had some fae blood.

The fae viewed the wisps as abominations—lost pieces of fae magic that didn't have enough life essence to coalesce into a being. They were considered soul-less, much like the ghouls. They floated across the face of the world searching for the lost part of themselves. Even if the elves didn't hold Thomas responsible for Faolan's actions, they'd never accept a wisp-made fae in their midst. James thought it was unlikely the elves would greet Thomas at their gates with anything other than an arrow through the heart.

Stalking prey through a city is much easier than stalking it through a forest. Freoric had no difficulty shadowing Thomas on the busy London streets. So many humans in one place provided more than enough cover. In the forest, it would not be so simple. Silence and stealth would be necessary. Here, it was easy enough to dress as a human, let his normally braided long hair flow instead over his shoulders to cover his ears, leave his bow behind in favor of a short, sharp knife, and feign disinterest as he walked along behind the human who strode along from shop to shop, making purchases along the way.

It took him by surprise when a slender young man who almost matched him in height fell into step with him and said, "I knew it would be an elf."

Freoric looked at the young man and recognized him as the man who shared space with his prey. He had soft blue eyes and brown hair, and his expression made him appear older than Freoric judged him to be. He continued walking.

The youth spoke again, "Thomas sensed someone had been following him. His magic is strong despite being only one-fourth fae. And who else would it be but an elf?"

Freoric stopped and turned to face the young man. "Go away. You don't interest me. I don't know you."

James knew that a geeky American boy was never going to impress an elven warrior. Freoric had at least two inches on him and the glint of silver in his hair told James that Freoric would have been ready for battle for at least a hundred years. "Your ancestors knew me when I was Myrddin."

Freoric stopped and turned to face the man who shared a living space with Thomas. "My ancestors respected Myrddin, but *I* don't know *you.*"

"Myrddin respected your ancestors. Me? I'm not thrilled to see you stalking my friend. Faolan has been dead for thousands of years. Thomas has no memories of being Faolan. All of that was wiped out when his amulet was destroyed to free the fae. Leave him alone. He isn't hurting you."

"He intended to kill all of the fae, the same as he murdered Myrddin. How can you defend him? He's an abomination."

"No. Not anymore. He practically worships the elves like he once worshipped the church. He's no danger to you."

"We'll decide that for ourselves."

"He's under my protection."

"As you say. I am only following him, for now. If I meant for him to be dead, he would be."

∗ ⌣ ∗ ⌣ ∗

James relaxed as he watched the elf round the corner in the opposite direction from the one Thomas had taken. He'd really bigged it up by playing the Myrddin card. He hoped the elves didn't realize that he had no natural magic. The best he could manage was mixing up herbs for natural remedies like any non-magic-wielding New Age health-food nut. He had all the knowledge, he just didn't have the stuff to back it up the way Myrddin had. He hustled through the crowd to catch up with his flat-mate.

As he fell into step with Thomas, Thomas looked over and said, "Who was it?"

"An elf, like I suspected. But I think they're only keeping an eye on you right now, not planning a full-on ninja assassination just yet."

"Faolan must have been a right old sod. We've only just rid ourselves of the monks that followed us here, and now I've got to worry about being mugged by my kin."

"Yeah, and only a month old, too," James grinned, enjoying his own running joke about Thomas's lack of memory, "I'm sure the elves aren't the only fae who'd like to have a go at you."

"Maybe we'd best get started working on protection spells instead of healing potions. How many pixie bites am I going to need to heal in London, anyway?"

"We may not be staying in London, if it's okay with you. I miss my friends and my stuff, to tell you the truth. Plus, Eamon's 'Underground money' is close to running out, and I can't get a job here because I can't get a work permit. I've got a job waiting for me back in Ohio, if I want it. Magical pest control is apparently set to become big business, and I could fit it in around school hours. That way I only miss a semester of college and can start back at the beginning of the year."

"And you want to see Lizbet," added Thomas, with a rare smile.

"Yes. And I want to see Lizbet," James said, smiling back.

"It would be nice to meet her," Thomas replied, "It would be nice to meet any of the other half-fae. I've no feelings for London one way or the other. I don't remember a life in England."

"Yeah, I don't know how she'd feel about that. Tanji—that's Lizbet's friend who's kind of related to me now through Myrddin—would be happy to meet you, I think. I'm not sure how strong her fae side's feelings are about Faolan, although she'd be..." James stopped and thought for a moment, "...his great aunt, Myrddin's sister. But if we end up back in the States, I don't know how Lizbet would feel about having you living right next door."

James stopped to examine a shop window sales banner. "But, the way I see it is this—Faolan murdered Myrddin, and if Myrddin doesn't hold it against you, Morgan and her other lives are going to have to let Lizbet alone about it sooner or later."

Forty-five minutes later, James slid the key into the lock of their shared flat as they arrived at the door. He walked into the flat and then abruptly stopped dead still. Thomas only stopped when he ran into James from behind. The small room was full of elves—a full council, by James's reckoning. It appeared that no one was much intimidated by Myrddin anymore.

A tall, grayed-haired elf folded his arms across his chest and nodded his head to James in the elven equivalent to "we come in peace." The other eight elves behind him stood unmoving, their arms also folded loosely across their chests.

James returned the greeting with the help of Myrddin's memories and asked, "Why are you here, Elder?"

The elves returned their hands to their sides, as did James.

"You have chosen to associate yourself with the man who imprisoned us for hundreds of years. Our ancient histories tell us you have always dealt respectfully with the elves, Myrddin, but we are unable to stay silent and let this wisp-endowed abomination practice magic near our families and our homes."

Thomas began to speak, "Elder...", but James held up a hand to stop him. Myrddin's memories were shoving at him hard not to let Thomas into the discussion. One wrong step and Thomas could lose his life so easily—as easily an as elf, with one liquid movement, can nock an arrow, draw a bow, and let the arrow fly.

"Elder, with respect, I ask that you call me by the name I wear in this life. If you can address me in the English tongue, then surely you can address me by my proper name. That name is James. Myrddin is with me, always, of course. I have his knowledge, his memories, and his influence. But I am not Myrddin as you knew him, just as Thomas is not Faolan."

"As you request, James, I recognize you are not entirely the man my ancestors knew. However, we know this man, this Thomas. We watched him from the other side. And the warrior we have had watching him on this side, Freoric, informs us that you are educating him in the way of sorcery and have placed him under your protection. We wonder why this is. He *is* Faolan."

"No longer. Your people saw what happened at the tree. Faolan is gone forever. I don't hold him responsible for what Faolan did any more than I hold you responsible for the actions of the elves who murdered Myrddin's father. Today, in this moment, there's only this empty-headed man behind me, cleared of memories and partially fae. Would you destroy an innocent?"

"If, as you say, Myrddin is with you, you know my people outlaw the mixing of human and elven blood. This has not changed," The elder nodded his head toward Thomas, "This one has no fae blood at all, he is only inhabited by a wisp, a contemptible thing. He is no kin of ours. However, we owe you a debt. If you have extended your protection, we will abide. What we will not tolerate is having him so near to us here on the green isle and on the continent beyond. In these times, for your people, it is easy to move from land to land. Find another place."

"And you won't follow us?" James asked.

"By my troth, the elves will not follow," replied the elder.

"I accept your troth. We'll leave before the new moon. Is that acceptable to you?"

"It is," the elder said, then folded his arms and nodded his head to indicate the meeting was over. The other elves directed the same greeting toward James and followed single file behind their council leader as he left the flat.

The last elf in line spat on the floor as he passed Thomas and mouthed, "Abomination."

James silently closed the door behind him as the elf moved into the hallway, then sucked in a deep gulp of air, and let it out sharply. "Wow...that was intense."

"You should have let me talk."

"No. Not a good idea. How can you not get that the only reason those guys haven't killed you is because they feel they owe a debt to Lizbet and me?" James felt his neck reddening as he let himself feel the anger he'd had to rein in tightly while he faced the elders.

"I could've eased their fears. I'm *for* the fae, I'm not Faolan. I'd defend them with my life...you know that. I want to live among them and learn from them."

James walked into the kitchen and plugged the kettle in for tea, needing movement to keep his anger from growing, "Look, Tom...it's not going to happen. They're never going to forget Faolan and forgive you, no matter how much you want it."

Thomas's eyes narrowed slightly before he responded, "And by the way, empty-headed?"

"You know what I meant," said James, "I defended you in a way the elves would accept. It seemed like a reasonable way of saying it at the time. I didn't do it to start a fight."

Thomas sat down at the small table in the corner of their shared kitchen. James set a cup in front of him, the tag of a tea bag trailing over the rim.

James said, "At least there's no more decision to make about going home. It's definitely time for us to get packing. We've got exactly seven days."

CHAPTER THREE

The Denial Twist

EAMON STOOD SILENTLY ON the crest of a small, green, Ohio hill, watching the grazing cows below. Although he was as at peace here as any gruagach could possibly be, a part of him was always alert, keeping his eyes and ears open for threats to the herd. He heard the lassie moving through the grass long before she got to him, and he knew her by her distinctive scent that was both human and elf.

Without turning around, he spoke quietly in his thick Scottish accent as she grew close, "So, Tanji, what brings you here on such a glorious day? Were you of a mind to spend some peaceful time with my little herd? Or...don't tell me...my mistress has changed her mind about my retirement and sent you to fetch me?"

"No, little dude, your mistress is busy kidding herself about what's going on inside her head. But anyone who knows Lizbet can tell there's something going on. She flipped out yesterday and looked like she was going to bash some gnome brains out while Bobby watched. That is not my Lizzie. That is also not the human Morgan or any of Lizbet's other ladies. That was the fae Morgan. I know it. And Langoureth knows it," Tanji said, as she sat down on a large rock near where Eamon stood. Sitting down put her only slightly above eye level with the standing gruagach.

"Agreed. I'd say the fae in her is growing restless. I didn't think she'd give up gracefully in the same way that Langoureth did for you. My mistress wouldn't have counted on the human personalities being the dominant ones after the remerge. She'll fight that to the bitter end. She would never content herself to be a set of memories and influences instead of being fully in charge."

"You know that, and I know that, but Lizbet is just like...in denial. I don't know how else to put it. I don't feel good about going behind her back, but you told me to let you know if anything looked fishy, and dude... it's become an all-fishies-into-the-pool situation."

"Lassie, don't put it all on the girl. She's being influenced by a powerful fae. Does she still have the wings?"

"Big, boss, beautiful wings, even though she doesn't want them."

"Right, see...fae don't have wings, except for the pixies and dragons who are just magical creatures. And they actually do need them for their flyin'. Among other fae, only Morgan has wings. An affectation-like that she adopted during Queen Victoria's time. She enjoyed her spyin' on the humans from the other realm and liked their twee pictorials of the fairy folk. Her wings are ornamental. Following the fashion, I suppose. She created and sustains them by a conscious act of magic. That means that she still has hold of the magic and is probably using every bit of it she can to influence and control Lizbet's thoughts."

"Lizzie still has super-mondo headaches. You think that's what's causing them?"

"Aye, probably. She's got a magically encapsulated fae in her brain. That has to hurt. The only ending I can see is that it'll eventually drive Lizbet mad, and my mistress will win dominance, or she'll just wear out and, again, my mistress will win dominance."

"I was kind of hoping for something better than a 'lose lose' proposition, Mr. Grim-To-The-Core. There has to be something we can do..."

"If I try to intervene, I fear what my mistress might do to the lass. I know she's in there listening all the time, even if it's not always obvious. Perhaps there's something you can do from that book I had sent from the old world? How much of it have you read?"

"A hundred or so pages. I keep getting distracted by spells I want to try. Plus, it's slow going. It takes a while with Langoureth's memories having to play translator for me."

"Are you pickin' up on the sorcery, then?"

Tanji waved her hand over a patch of wildflowers with buds that were yet to bloom and spoke a few quiet words. As she did, the flowers sprung to full bloom instantly. Tanji smiled and nodded. "I've got a good start. I seem to have a talent for making things grow."

"Good. You may need some magic before this is through. Although I recommend you focus on spells for healing and protection. I can't really see a few bloomin' flowers setting Morgan to shakin' in her boots."

"Yeah, well...I'd rather just help Lizbet before she gets taken over and not have to prepare for a war."

"I don't know how to help her, lass. It's Lizbet's battle now. We might be able to influence and scheme, but in the end, Lizbet will have to beat the queen with her own strength. I know her, and I believe she can win, but Morgan is a strong force. How else could a nymph become queen? Nymphs, even those whose magic gives them the power of the aether, are not generally considered by the fae when choosing their leaders. Morgan has been a notable exception."

"Yeah, that's another thing. The gnomes kept yelling, 'the queen, the queen', so I think they can tell that Morgan took over Lizbet, too."

"Aye, she never liked gnomes. They all fear her. You need to understand...Morgan, for hundreds of years, was a good queen. She united the fae after Faolan sent them to the shadow realm. Without her, the stresses of living that way might well have overwhelmed them. She has great power over the fae, particularly now that she's freed them as she promised she would do. But I'd rather Lizbet wield that power than see it continue to rest in the hands of the bitter, angry creature my Morgan has become."

"I don't think Lizbet would want that kind of responsibility. She just wants things to be like they were before she went to Scotland. She doesn't like being 'the girl with wings' who everybody wants a piece of."

"Believe me, there's no one who understands wantin' to be released from duties more than I do, but there's a lack of leadership among the fae now and old rivalries are heating up. They're all breakin' into factions, and with the fae, that always ends in war. Not much different from humans, I suppose. They need their queen to keep things stabilized, and like it or no, that queen is either Morgan or Lizbet. I know you think it doesn't concern you, but any war coming among the fae can't help but threaten humans."

Sheila Moore dried the dishes she'd already washed and stacked in the draining rack. Lizbet had a headache again, and Sheila didn't have the heart to keep her daughter on her chore routine when she was so clearly in pain. She'd had Lizbet to doctors several times, but they had found nothing wrong with her despite all the tests. Sheila worried for her. Ever since she'd returned from Scotland she was not only physically different, with chronic headaches and well...wings, but the joy had gone out of her. Lizbet had always been such an upbeat, happy, active girl.

As Sheila worked through the small stack of dishes, her gaze drifted out the back window and into the garden, where a small group of gnomes hoisted one of the ceramic garden gnome statues up above their heads and began to carry it across the garden. They dropped it several times, raising their voices and throwing punches at each other each time they did.

Sheila left the dishes to dry themselves and moved to the sliding glass door that opened on to the back patio to get a better look. She'd tried to remove the ceramic gnomes several times, but she couldn't budge them. She also couldn't figure out how they were held down; there were no obvious stakes or cement that could hold them fixed in place.

She was surprised when the gnomes finally made it to the back of the garage where they managed to knock the lid off one of the garbage cans and, with the only well-co-ordinated effort of their task, toss the gnome statue up and into the can. Afterward, they ran quickly back to the garden and started all over again with the next one. They didn't stop until they had removed all seven of them. It took nearly an hour.

When the job was complete, they ran onto the patio and looked up at her, each of them saying one of two words.

She understood the first. It was "Bobby."

She didn't understand the second, gnomish word.

Sheila turned and called for her son. "Bobby, you have guests..."

~~*

Bobby was immersed in a video game when his mother called for him. "I'm busy, mom."

"Well, you're going to have to tell your little gnome friends that. They're all standing around on the patio asking for you, and I don't think they have any plans to go away."

"Alright..." Bobby saved his game and headed toward the back door. When the gnomes saw him, they cheered.

As he exited the house, two of the gnomes climbed up his body and perched themselves on his shoulders as the others led him back to the burrow.

This was something new. He went out to see what the gnomes were doing a lot, but they had never come for him.

When they got him into the garden, Gurrdenn called up to him, "Sit, Bobby, sit."

Bobby sat. The gnomes formed into a circle around him, serious expressions on their dirt-smeared faces. Each one of them wore a hat made from the face of a small bird or animal. Even though Bobby had told them not to use it for fur, the neighbor's former cat was represented in the circle.

Gurrdenn made a speech in gnomish that Bobby didn't understand and then handed him a wreath of twigs, miming for Bobby to place it on his head. After Bobby set the wreath on top of his red curls, the gnomes began to dance around him, eventually laughing, farting, and whirling with their usual glee. Whatever serious moment had just happened was now over. Bobby got up, touched Gurrdenn on the arm, saying "Tag, you're it!", and the games began.

The fae Morgan opened her eyes into the darkness of Lizbet's room. The girl had gone to bed early again with one of her headaches. Good. More time for Morgan.

She stood the girl up, enjoying the feel of her young, athletic body, so different from the elderly body she had been burdened with when the realms were separated. Morgan was glad to have remerged with a human half that was so young. She hadn't counted on the girl being such a fighter, but she had managed to preserve her separateness when the remerge occurred through the skillful application of magic and sheer will. Lizbet experienced her only as a painful buzzing in her naive, young brain.

Morgan walked to the closet and exchanged the girl's pajamas for a long, velveteen dress. She moved to the full-length mirror on the wall and smiled. Myrddin, when he saw her again, would be hard pressed to resist her. She'd be with him soon enough; she knew it, as surely as she knew that the strength of the girl was failing more and more each day. She didn't actively wish the girl harm, but now that she could be with Myrddin again after all this time, she had no choice but to remove her as a competitor.

Morgan opened the window, smelled deeply of the clean night air, then slowly faded into the aether. Moments later she arrived in London, coalescing again to float lightly outside the window of James's bedroom. It was dark, but not so dark that she couldn't make out his figure tangled in the bedclothes. She stayed to watch him sleep until his alarm rang and he rolled over, opened his eyes, and sleepily reached out to turn it off. She had missed him so terribly for so long, and to have Myrddin again so close...

As she faded back into the aether to take the girl's body home, she thought he might have caught a glimpse of her. But never mind, he would only think her a dream he pulled into reality from his sleep. Soon, though, she would be able to be with him in more than his dreams.

Broken Wings

LIZBET WOKE TO THE sound of her alarm, exhausted rather than well-rested. Every morning now she felt like she'd hardly slept at all. She didn't know how much longer she could keep going. The headaches, the exhaustion—and yesterday she'd blanked out completely, waking up to find herself standing in the garden, holding a couple of gnomes upside down, with Bobby standing in front of her looking terrified.

Why can't it just go back to how it was? she thought as she headed for the bathroom. She remembered why as she caught the first glimpse of herself in the mirror. *Because of the freaking wings. I'm marked.*

It's not that they weren't pretty. They were gorgeous; not too big, not too small, feathery and mostly blue, tipped with colorful "eyes" like a peacock tail. They shimmered where the light hit them. She understood why Tanji liked them so much, but when Lizbet had imagined fairies as a child, she'd imagined their wings as small, gauzy things, not at all like the solid, muscular protrusions set in her upper back. And comfort? Sure, there are *lots* of comfortable ways to lie down or sit when you've got wings. Thinking about leaning your back up against a wall? Forget it.

Her wings were about one and a half feet across when fully furled, as they often were when she was angry, upset, or the headache was at its most painful level. They were not really broad enough to be terrifying to an attacker even if she had also grown talons and a sharp beak. No, they were just big enough to distract people from what she was trying to say. Sometimes her father could barely look at her.

It might have been a little more okay if flapping her wings actually produced a little flight time, but she had tried and...nothing. She'd felt like she might take off a couple of times when she'd tripped and been off balance, but she couldn't manage to fly even a couple of feet with a running start. She looked fae, but she didn't control her magic. Magical things sometimes happened around her, but she never made them happen.

Lizbet took a quick shower and got dressed. She would have liked to have dressed in something new for her first day of school, but it's difficult to shop when you have to accommodate an extra set of appendages. It seemed to be part of the magic she inherited that her clothes would re-tailor themselves to fit over the wings, but she'd had to pay for a few things she didn't want when they re-tailored themselves in the store. They weren't even things she could see herself wearing. They were too mature and fancy for her. She was happy with jeans, yoga pants, baby tees, or cotton button-downs over a cami. She didn't need the glam dresses in fancy fabrics she'd felt compelled to try on.

Being in the mall had made her feel like she was on display. People pointed, gawked, and turned to friends to talk about her. It had just been too much. She'd eventually turned and asked her mom if they could just go home, and she hadn't tried going to the mall again. It couldn't go on that way forever. She would have to get new clothes eventually, but she hoped that before her clothes weren't wearable anymore, she'd have lost the fairy extras.

But today, right after breakfast, she had to face going to school in last year's clothes with a brand new, shiny set of wings.

* ~ * ~ *

"Hey, Moore! Take off your backpack and show me your wings."

Bobby turned around to see who was yelling at him. It was one of the big boys from fifth grade. The boy started to move fast toward where Bobby stood on the sidewalk in front of school.

"I don't have wings. That's my sister."

"Yeah? I don't believe you. Gimme your backpack and let's see," the older boy said as he grabbed the strap of Bobby's bag and tried to pull it off of his shoulder. Bobby hung on, his small body tight with the effort, but the boy was stronger than he was, and he pulled the bag away with a couple of strong tugs.

"Give it back! It's not yours!" Bobby yelled, but the boy pushed against Bobby's chest and held the bag away from him with his other hand.

"Show me your wings, Moore. Come on!"

Then the boy screamed. Gurrdenn had gotten the zipper

clasp undone, crawled out of the bag unto the boy's arm, and dug sharp teeth into his wrist.

Bobby laughed aloud. "Gurrdenn! When did you get in there?" Gurrdenn kept right on chewing.

The boy dropped the backpack, screaming and slapping at the gnome, "Get him off me, get him off me."

"Stop, Gurrdenn! He let it go," Bobby told the gnome, and Gurrdenn dropped to the ground, making room for the boy to run quickly away.

"And don't ever pick on me again, or I'll have all my gnomes come after you!" Bobby yelled at the fleeing boy's back.

~~*

"Girl, you're beautiful, you're strong, and you can do this," Tanji reassured Lizbet while she carefully pulled the car into a narrow space in the school parking lot. "If anyone says anything, you just give them that trademark Moore snark right back."

"If you say so. But Tanj...I'm just so tired."

"I know, but you can make it through today, I know you can. Look, my life was complicated enough being half black and half white. The white kids know I'm not one of them, and once the black kids meet my dad, suddenly I'm not black anymore, either. Throw being half fae into the mix, and try to tell me that things could be more complicated! So, we're both freaks. Who cares? Let everybody get a good gander at you, and then it can only get better from here."

The two girls walked up the steps toward the school door. One of the boys who leaned up against the railing made a flapping movement with his arms and yelled out,

"Nice pair!" The other boys in the group laughed and high-fived him.

Tanji kept her eyes straight ahead as they walked and said quietly, "Ignore it. If you'd ridden your bike to school, one of those jerks would have said, 'nice rack' when you were locking it up in the bike rack. You know that. They're fools."

The two girls continued up the stairs and into the open doorway, and as they walked down the hall to Lizbet's locker, everyone got quieter as they approached, elbowing their friends and turning to watch Lizbet and Tanji as they came down the hall. Then, as they passed, they heard the whispering start behind them.

Tanji suddenly raised her hands above her head in a flourish and slowly turned in a circle. She'd worn her hair up so that her elven ears were clearly visible. "Alright, alright, I know you're all looking at the ears, going 'mmmhhhmmm, wish I could rock me a set of ears the way that girl rocks 'em', but you *know* nobody can rock 'em like me." Tanji struck a series of glam-girl poses while the other students either laughed along with her or turned away, suddenly embarrassed that they'd been staring. Several people shouted encouragement with "you go, girl" and "looking good!"

Tanji hooked her arm through Lizbet's and pulled her down the hall, both of them laughing so hard that they were gasping for air, ears and wings forgotten as they just enjoyed each other's company.

They got to Lizbet's locker, and when Lizbet was able to catch her breath, she said, "Tanj...you are a freak, but you are *my* freak."

～～*

Sheila Moore felt like she was back in grade school as she sat in one of the kid-sized plastic chairs in the elementary school principal's office, waiting to be called in for her appointment. She had never had problems with either of her children's behavior at school, so the experience was something new for her. She couldn't imagine that Bobby would start a fight with another child. Despite his blazing red hair, he was never temperamental.

Sheila stood as gracefully as she could when the secretary advised her that the Principal would see her. Bobby was already in the office, looking like he was about to cry. Her boy was so tender-hearted. There was no way that sweet child would have gotten into a fight if he had any other choice.

Principal Connors stood up and gestured to the empty seat next to Bobby. "I'd have liked to have met you under different circumstances, Mrs. Moore. Normally, Bobby is such a well-behaved student."

Sheila replied, "I understood from the secretary who called my office that Bobby was in a fight?"

Bobby quickly chimed in, "I didn't fight anyone..."

Principal Connors looked over the top of her glasses at him, "Bobby, it's my turn to talk now."

Bobby folded his arms and lowered his head.

"Yes, technically, Bobby didn't fight anyone. He brought a gnome to school to do his fighting for him. One of the fifth grade boys has some very nasty bites on his arm. I'm sure he's going to need a tetanus booster and possibly rabies shots."

"How terrible! I'm so sorry..."

"I have no choice but to suspend Bobby for the next week due to the seriousness of the issue. You can pick up each day's work after school, and he can complete it at home."

"But he's never done anything like this before. And I don't think the gnomes actually listen to anyone. Even if they did, Bobby wouldn't have told a gnome to attack another child."

"We don't allow violence or *magic* in this school, Mrs. Moore. You may have different rules at your home, but we have high standards here. He's suspended for one week. If he brings a gnome or any other magical creature to school again after that, he'll be expelled."

Sheila stood up, "I understand. Lizbet will pick up the work from his teacher after school each day, if that's okay."

"No, it's *not* okay for Lizbet to pick up his work. As I said...there is to be no magic in the school. Your daughter has wings, Mrs. Moore. She is clearly practicing magic."

"Fine," Sheila said, beginning to burn on the inside while remaining calm on the outside, "His father or I will pick up his work. Come on, Bobby."

On the way to the car, Bobby told his mother, "I didn't fight anyone. The kid tried to take my backpack 'cause he said he wanted to see my wings, and Gurrdenn jumped out and just started biting him. I didn't even know he was in there."

"I believe you, Bobby," Sheila said curtly, still working hard for control.

Bobby couldn't hear everything his mother said to his father when she called him at work, but he knew that she was angry—maybe even angrier than she'd ever been. He hid around the corner in the hallway while his parents talked on the phone.

"Steven, I'm furious about the whole thing..." his mother

said. Bobby put his head on his knees and hugged them tightly to his chest. He began to rock just a little, but he told himself he wouldn't cry.

"Well, something needs to be done. It's not acceptable..."

His mother's voice grew quieter and he couldn't hear her for a little while.

"... but can you take him?"

"Yes, call me back when you know. Thank you, Steve..."

Bobby started to cry quietly. Now he was even going to be sent away.

"Bobby?" his mother called, then walked into the hall-way and nearly fell over the weeping boy as she rounded the corner.

"Please don't send me away. I didn't do it, really. I didn't do it!" he managed between sobs.

His mother collapsed to the floor and pulled him close to her, nearly bursting into tears herself. "Oh Bobby, I'm not mad at you...I'm mad at lots of people, but I'm not mad at you. Your father isn't mad at you, either. That's not why I asked him to let you stay there. It's because you can't stay home alone. I can't have time off work until later in the week. Someone has to be able to stay with you while you're suspended. Your father is sometimes able to work from home, that's why I asked him if you could stay there." She smoothed his hair and pulled him even closer.

Bobby sniffled a few more times and said, "Are you sure?"

"Honey, I'm completely sure. I know that you wouldn't do what the Principal said you did, and I know you would never lie to me about it even if you did do it. If that Principal thinks that gnomes don't have minds of their own, then she has obviously never met a gnome! And to say that Lizbet is practicing magic because of something she has no control over..." His mom took a deep breath and then let it out slowly. "She's just wrong, Bobby, and it made me mad. But that's between adults, not between you and the principal, okay? I don't want you getting angry and getting in trouble again."

"Yeah, okay, mom." Bobby snuggled into his mother's arms and stopped crying.

CHAPTER FIVE

I Will Follow Him

GURRDENN MOTIONED MESHHARR, GORJUNN, and Kaluum to follow him. They were unusually silent for gnomes. Below the window, they formed a gnome pyramid and Gurrdenn scrambled to the top. He could see Bobby inside, sitting down and watching a picture box. A man, the father, entered the room and sat down next to him.

Gurrdenn jumped down and looked around, trying to figure out how the huddle could build a burrow on the hard walkway, high in the air, so far away from the yielding earth.

Bobby called to his father, "Can I watch TV?"

Mr. Moore walked into the small living room and joined

Bobby on the couch. "Looks like you've already turned it on without asking. Don't you have any schoolwork?"

"No. You have to pick it up from my teacher after school, remember?"

"Yes, I remember. But being suspended from school shouldn't be a vacation. I'm trying to think if there are any chores you could do until you have some homework..."

"But..."

"No buts, Bobby. I know you didn't start that fight, but did you try to stop the gnome from hurting that boy?"

"No...but..."

"Bobby, gnomes aren't pets. I don't know what they are, but they're definitely not pets. I've told you that I don't like you playing with them even though your mother doesn't seem to mind. I don't feel safe about you being around magical creatures."

"But Lizzie is magical, too!"

"Lizzie has an...affliction. Lizzie is different," Steve said, but in his heart, he knew that he had real concerns about what his daughter had become. He hated himself for it, but he didn't feel comfortable with Lizbet's wings, Tanji's ears, the gnomes, pixies, or any of the other fae and magical creatures he'd heard about. He also didn't like that mouthy gruagach Lizbet treated like an old friend. If he had his way, she'd be forbidden to associate with it.

Out of the corner of his eye, Steve saw movement. He looked toward the picture window, and he saw something disappearing from view at the bottom of the frame as he turned. He walked to the window and looked down. *Gnomes. Filthy, disgusting gnomes.*

"Unbelievable! Bobby, are these the gnomes from your mom's house?" He motioned to Bobby to come to the window and take a look.

Bobby moved to the window and looked down at the gnomes. They looked back up at him, giant grins lighting all of their faces when they saw him, "Yeah, that's Gurrdenn, Kaluum, and...I don't say the names of the other ones right."

"Do they always follow you like this?"

"I guess so. Gurrdenn got into my backpack yesterday, and I didn't know he was there. I told you I didn't mean to take him to school. See? Now you know it's true."

The gnomes called out to Bobby and motioned for him to come play. They began a game that looked similar to tag but also included apparently friendly slaps and kicks. Because they were gnomes, flatulence was involved.

How can anyone stand this? thought Steven. He took out his cell and dialed a number that had been playing on the local radio station for days. "Hello. Yes, is that Ron? This is Steve Moore, Lizbet's father, and you can definitely help me...I'd like to arrange for a gnome removal."

By the second day of school, Lizbet felt better than she had since Fae Day. She didn't have a headache, and when she woke up, she felt fully rested for the first time in a long time. Tanji had been right—the first day of school had been rough, but a lot of people had gotten over the novelty of her wings by the end of the day. Now most people were interacting with her pretty much the same way they always had. It was okay to be at school when no one was staring at her.

"Hey, Moore- you going out for track this year?" A friend from last year's team called out from behind while hurrying to catch up.

"Nah," Lizbet replied, "Not so much into the athletic kick this year. I thought I'd focus on my studies."

"Man, that's too bad. You were one of our strongest runners for relay."

"Yeah, whatever. Just not into it anymore, I guess." She didn't want to tell anyone the truth because it hurt too much to talk about it. At the end of the day before, the track coach had sought her out to tell her that the school district administration had voted unanimously to disallow "magically altered" students from competing on the teams. It really stung her when the coach she looked up to practically told her she thought Lizbet was a freak.

Not that the coach was wrong about her. She *was* a freak. She wished she could take it in stride like Tanji did, even embrace it, but she couldn't.

At least she still had her bike to get a workout if she couldn't be on a team, and she was riding to dad's after school to see Bobby. She hadn't realized how much Bobby had gotten lost in the shuffle in the past month, and she felt bad about that when her mother mentioned it in her gentle way. She also realized she would be feeling better about everything if she'd been spending time with her brother, being normal, instead of sitting around feeling sorry for herself. Bobby's joyful approach to life could always cheer her up on a bad day.

The bike ride to school that morning had gone a long way to clear her head and give her some perspective. She was going to make some changes, and the first one was to make sure Bobby knew she hadn't ditched him.

Thomas watched James from the window of their flat. James had popped out to the shops on his own to purchase their dinner, but he was never truly on his own anymore. Three wisps trailed behind him, causing the sidewalk to clear of human traffic around him as he walked. No one wanted to come in contact with the wisps.

The wisps looked the way most people imagined ghosts looked: ephemeral, a milky blue-white, and transparent, no more than a foot wide and three or four feet long. But they weren't ghosts. Each wisp had a small living essence in addition to the magic leftover from the body of a partial fae.

Usually, the wisps floated randomly with no apparent purpose, searching for the feel of their missing half among the humans so that they could be corporeal again. Thomas could feel the magic in them all the time when they were near.

James said he couldn't feel their magic, but they were drawn to him just the same. He thought it was because they could sense Myrddin's memories inside him, and those memories were missing the magic that had once been a part of him. Thomas believed that if James were to open himself to the wisps, they could merge with him, and he would have natural magic again.

James wouldn't discuss it, but Thomas was sure that if James really remembered what he was passing up, he'd change his mind. All he needed was to feel the energizing, electric glow of magic investing the cells of his body again. James had helped Thomas start a new life after he lost his memories. It had become Thomas's fondest desire to give James back the gift of magic in return.

~~*

When Lizbet got to her English class and slid into the seat next to Tanji, her friend said, "Eamon says hi. You should go visit him."

"When did you see Eamon?"

"Yesterday. He's helping me with some stuff for the blog I'm doing for Dad's business. Dad says the business shouldn't just be about 'pest control' but also about helping people understand magic and what to do when they come across either a potentially dangerous or potentially friendly new beastie. I think it's great! But...I do need some help, so I hunted Eamon down and dragged him away from the cows for a while."

"He's still hanging out with those cows? Last time I saw him, he said he wanted to go back to Scotland."

"Yeah, I don't know why he's still hanging around here... especially since his great bud Lizbet never visits. But he did mention getting back to the other gruagachs sooner or later. I think he's lonely," Tanji said, "So that's why you should go see him."

"I can't tonight. I promised I'd go see Bobby for a while. He's really upset about what happened at school. I guess Mom thinks he was hanging out with the gnomes so much because the rest of us weren't paying any attention to him. So, I kind of feel responsible for what happened."

"Yeah, you kind of feel responsible for everything lately," Tanji said as the teacher arrived and the class quieted.

$$* \sim * \sim *$$

Lizbet strained her way up The Hill, wishing she hadn't stopped riding for so long. The Hill took a much bigger toll on her muscles and motivation than usual, but she resisted the temptation to make it easier by getting off and walking.

She took a moment at the top of The Hill to rest and look upward at the hawks gliding on the air currents above, envying them the easy use of their wings. Then she crossed the road, threw her leg over her bike again, and gave a few quick turns on the pedals before she stood up with one hand out to the breeze to coast down the long, steep slope.

Flying. That's what the coast down the hill feels like. No wings needed. It was the one awesome thing she could count on when everything else in her life was wrong—that moment when she felt like she was flying.

And then she realized that there was more than coasting going on—her feet lifted off the pedals, and she no longer felt the seat beneath her although she still held the bike with one hand. Then she had to let the handlebar go as the front wheel left the ground and she lifted off the bike completely. She watched her precious bike bounce into the weeds at the side of the path and topple over, then come to a stop, but she was still moving on the air, free as a hawk.

Her wings didn't flap, although they were spread wide as they often were without any conscious action on her part. Obviously, it didn't matter that her wings were useless. She was flying without them.

Eamon stood at the bottom of the hill, watching the girl descend and then start to rise as her bike fell away beneath her. He muttered to himself, "Fine time to take charge of the magic..."

Eamon ran below her on the path and yelled up to her. "Are ye alright, then? Have control of the situation-like?"

"No, I do *not* have control of the situation-like! How do I stop?"

"Aim for a soft spot, lass...I see one—follow me!"

Eamon headed for a patch of swampy ground just off the path. The sodden moss underneath squished and sucked at his feet, but he kept running until he found the driest spot and called the girl to him, "Alright, lass, focus on coming toward me."

Lizbet veered slightly toward him, but she took her eyes off him for a moment and traveled back up, following the direction of her gaze.

"Keep your eyes on me now, and think about comin' down. Just gently, gently..." Eamon watched as the girl's flight slowed, and she shifted toward where he was standing. The descent looked awkward, her wings slapping about now but not in a way that seemed to be helpful.

"That's right, lass, focus only on me and think about how you'll be standing here having a conversation in just a moment."

Lizbet slowed, and her feet moved toward the earth as she continued on her uneven flight toward Eamon.

"That's right, put down the landing gear and reach out toward the earth..." Eamon jumped out of the way as one of Lizbet's feet hit the ground a few feet in front of him but her body kept coming forward. She flopped into the moss with a wet whump and pushed herself up on her hands to reveal a face full of muddy water.

She broke into a broad grin. "That was the most amazing thing I've ever done! How do I do it again?"

"I couldn't tell ye. Why not just try?" asked Eamon.

She stood up and took a few steps, and then flew a couple of feet before she landed in the mud again. This time, it was a gentler landing.

"Now, I'm no expert on this, mind, but perhaps you should think lifting more than rolling-like, do ye know what I mean—helicopter take off instead of plane? That might give a better landing."

"A better landing would be good." Lizbet stood up

straight with an expression of concentration, her eyebrows rising just a little, as if they could lift her up all by themselves. She rose slightly and hung there. Then she moved forward and back again. With a smile on her face, she turned and flew higher into the sky, going straight up in a controlled spiral.

Eamon smiled when he heard her raucous laughter from above. No doubt about it, he hadn't been wrong about this one. This girl, covered in mud and howling like a banshee, was born to be fae.

CHAPTER SIX

Come Fly With Me

L IZBET CALLED BOBBY'S CELL and said, "Hey runt, come outside. I'm here." Then she looked up and followed in the direction that she gazed. When she reached the balcony and her head crested over the railing, the gnomes that were sitting with their backs to the wall under the picture window of the apartment looked up in fright, jumping to their feet, ready to fight. They lost interest quickly after they identified her, muttering in gnomish, "not the queen, not the queen." Lizbet understood what they said and realized they had mistaken her for Morgan. She thought it was odd that they would do that. The fae had been in her nineties when she'd split from the human Morgan, and, according to Eamon, she'd been stuck with her elderly appearance in the shadow realm.

When Bobby opened the apartment door, Lizbet was hanging in the air on the far side of the second-floor-walkway railing, fluttering her wings a little bit just for the effect. She was beginning to understand that flight and direction was simply a matter of will.

Bobby gaped. "No way! You're flying!"

"Yep, I'm flyin'. And it's super cool. When you're not grounded anymore, we can see if I'm strong enough to take you for a ride, too. The flying Moores! Woohoo!"

"NO!" Lizbet's father growled as he appeared in the doorway, pulling Bobby behind him and away from her, "Elizabeth, get away from him. Go home. I don't want him around magic. I've had enough. Your mother may put up with this, but I won't."

Lizbet's head started to pound, and she realized she was losing control of the magic that kept her afloat. She began to drop toward the ground a story below, picking up speed as she went. She landed hard, twisting an ankle when she lost her balance as she hit the grass.

She heard her father's voice call down to her from the balcony, "Are you okay?"

"I'm okay, dad. I think I twisted my ankle, though." Lizbet looked up to the balcony where her father peered over with a look of disgust twisting his features. Her heart ached. She had expected to see concern.

"Good. Nothing serious, then. I'll call your mother to pick you up. You need to stay away from Bobby until you realize that magic is dangerous and wrong."

"But dad..."

"You heard me."

"Okay, fine, but don't call mom. I'll call Tanji and ask her for a ride home. Mom doesn't need any more worries!" Lizbet used the pillar of one of the columns that held up the walkway to carefully get herself up onto her good foot. She checked out the ankle with a tentative step and immediately withdrew her weight from it.

Lizbet didn't want Mom to see Dad this way. She was stressed out enough as it was with Bobby's suspension. And, maybe, Lizbet was a little bit afraid that her mother would take her father's side this time.

Thomas sat pondering in the light of a small desktop lamp after having reviewed all of James's notes about the spells Myrddin thought he should learn. None of them would help him to put magic back into someone who no longer had it.

Wasn't getting magic back a form of healing? To him, it was. If James had that knowledge, he should share it. But he also knew that he couldn't ask James for it. He knew that James didn't see himself as broken or lacking in any way without magic.

James had made it clear in their long, late-night discussions that he thought of magic differently than Thomas did: he saw it as academically interesting, something that he could study. He didn't see it as a way of life he should be living.

James was Thomas's only friend. As far as he knew, the only friend he'd ever had. Thomas wanted James to be able to feel the same passion he did for magic. He wanted James to understand the pure physical connection to the elements that magic gave its host. It was an amazing feeling, and it lifted you above the mundane people all around. It was such a gift that James surely couldn't refuse it if it were given to him.

It was really just a question of how to cause James's body to absorb the magic of a few of the wisps that were so drawn to him. He'd thought about it for days, and sitting pondering in near darkness wasn't bringing him any nearer to sorting it...but then...it was easy, wasn't it? Why hadn't he cottoned to it before? It was so simple, and it only required a small trick to accomplish. James would forgive him the trick later when he was once again the powerful sorcerer Myrddin had been. Thomas was sure of it: James would want to be healed, even if he had to be tricked into it.

He wondered if he had time to prepare his gift before they left for the States. He headed for the kitchen and his ever increasing cache of potions.

Lizbet popped the front tire off her bike, and Tanji stowed both pieces in the trunk of her car. Lizbet limped around to the passenger side door, carefully arranging her warm-up jacket across the seat before sitting down so she didn't get mud on the upholstery.

"I think I can do something about your ankle," Tanji said as she slid into the driver's seat, "Let's go out to the park before I take you home and find a quiet place where I can focus."

"You mean you can heal it?"

"Maybe. I've been dying for a real human to practice my voodoo on."

"Sure, okay. I guess I trust you on this. Can you heal my dad's screwed up head, too? I really don't know what's up with him. He basically told me that I can't see Bobby until I stop having anything to do with magic. It's not like I can suddenly stop being half-fae." Lizbet's head was pulsing fiercely with the pain now, "And do you think you can do anything about my achy head?"

"I'm pretty sure I can't do anything about your head. I keep telling you, that's not a normal headache. Until you realize that ol' fae is in there making trouble, you're not going to beat her...I am sorry about your dad, though. My parents have been superstars about everything. Not that my mom has been around anymore than usual. But when I see her, she's cool with it."

"My dad has always been strict, but..."

"Just say it, girl. It sucks."

"Yep. It definitely does."

"Okay, so...we're here," Tanji said as she pulled into a parking spot at the park, "Think you can hobble into the woods a little way with my help? I feel more focused with the magic when I'm away from technology and out in nature."

Lizbet opened the car door and gingerly lifted herself up, favoring her healthy leg. "Yeah, I'm good...but not too far, right?"

"There's a really nice spot through here. It's just a short walk. This is more of a game trail than a path, so we'll have to take it slow." Tanji walked to Lizbet, who threw an arm around Tanji's shoulders, and the girls moved slowly along the path together with Lizbet trying not to wince each time her sore ankle got jostled.

After about ten minutes, the path opened to a small, sunlit meadow, and Tanji helped lower Lizbet to the ground. Lizbet crossed her legs, and Tanji sat across from her in the same position.

"Okay, so...first, drink this," Tanji said, handing Lizbet a bottle she'd taken from her backpack, "It's just some herbs and things, but they make your body more receptive to the magic."

Lizbet drank the contents of the bottle, grimacing as she did. "Tastes like toilet."

Tanji grinned. "Thought it might. Couldn't make me drink it! Okay, so, close your eyes and clear your head. No talking from here on out. I've got focusing to do."

Lizbet did as she was instructed, and Tanji closed her eyes, too, quietly chanting in the old tongue, the one that Langoureth had known. As she chanted, Tanji held her hands palm up in front of her. After a moment, she opened her eyes and reached out to place her hands on Lizbet's ankle. A soft blue glow briefly lit Lizbet's skin where Tanji touched as she moved her hands over the injured tissues. Then the light dimmed and finally extinguished.

"Okay, I think that's got it. Open your eyes and let's find out if you can stand on your own now."

Lizbet uncrossed her legs and tentatively started to stand. Soon, she was upright. She walked a few steps, not limping, and then looked back to her friend, "How did you learn to do that?"

"I got Langoureth's spell book a couple of weeks ago."

"Really? How'd you get it?" Lizbet asked as the girls started the walk back to the car, moving much more quickly than they had when they left it.

"I knew where it was because of Langoureth banging around in here," Tanji said as she tapped her temple with one finger, "but I didn't have any way to get it. So, I mentioned it to Eamon, and he knew all about it. He got a message to a gruagach friend in Scotland named Hamish, and Hamish went to where Langoureth kept it hidden. Apparently, it was a place you visited when you were there—Dumbarton Castle? Hamish defused the magical booby trap Langoureth had set using the instructions I gave him, and he was able to get the book without too much trouble. And then he FedExed it to me."

Lizbet laughed. "How weird does that sound? '...and then the fairy FedExed it to me'. No magical enchantment, no secret spells or fairy dust, just FedEx. Have you done a lot of spells from the book?"

"A few. It seems like I have a talent for growing things, which has something to do with healing, I guess. Stuff that's really connected to nature. Eamon says that I have elf magic, which forms itself naturally around both war and healing because elves get into wars a lot and that means they need fixing up a lot. Some elves have a talent for dangerous magic that they use to make their arrows fly true. Others have a talent for sensing their enemies, kind of like James told you Thomas can sense all of the magic around him. He's got elf magic, too, so that makes sense."

"James says that I should have nymph magic, and specifically, the talents of the celestial nymphs, the aureas, who can move through the aether."

"Yeah, the fae Morgan loved using that to drop in from nowhere when you weren't expecting her, according to lots of Langoureth's memories. I guess she couldn't do it when she was human, so maybe you won't be able to either. But...I'm kind of looking for something specific in the book right now to do a favor for Eamon." Tanji hoped she didn't look as shady as she felt when she said that, knowing Lizbet wouldn't be pleased with Tanji hiding something from her. "It's slow going. It's a huge book, and the translation takes me a while. But, really, the words, they're for focusing more than anything, so sometimes it doesn't really matter whether or not I understand them."

Tanji suddenly realized that if Morgan was sitting around in Lizbet's head, listening in, she had the perfect way to draw her out. "You know that Morgan must have had a spell book somewhere, and you should be able to get it if you remember where it was. I mean, so where is it? Mine's right there on top of my dresser every night, so that's easy enough to get my hands on."

"There's no book as far as I know, so I'm not going to be digging up some big trove of knowledge any time soon. The human Morgan kept all her knowledge in her head, so the fae Morgan may have done that, too."

"That's too bad. Then again, Morgan was always jealous of Langoureth's knowledge. Maybe Morgan's book wouldn't have made the grade." Tanji couldn't resist the dig, knowing the fae was spying on her every word.

After Tanji dropped Lizbet home, she pulled around the corner and parked so that she could pull out her phone and let Eamon know what she'd done. She was going to need his help if things went wrong.

~~*

Ron parked the truck across two spaces. "Ron Ross's Humane Gnome Removal (and Magical Creature Control)" was emblazoned in bright red letters across the side of the truck just above a cartoon of a smiling gnome entering a cozy-looking cabin among a bed of well-tended flowers.

From the second floor balcony, Steve Moore called down to him, "Ron, good to see you again. How's business?"

Ron looked up. "Good, Steve, good. It's been a while. Lizbet hasn't been around to the house much, either. Tanji says she's still not feeling well?"

"Lizbet is a whole other topic. Right now, I've got a gnome problem to take care of."

Ron could see the gnomes had made themselves at home

on the balcony as soon as he topped the stairs. They'd filled the side of the walkway below the apartment's picture window with bundles of cardboard and built a makeshift burrow. "Odd for them to be so far away from a garden or a garden center."

"You take these gnomes out of here, and then stop by my wife's house and round up the rest of the huddle there. That's the job, okay? I don't want to have to deal with them anymore."

Ron was surprised by the man's brusqueness, but he knew that a lot of people were having a problem getting comfortable with the strange new world of creatures. "Got it. Just thinking out loud. Need to develop a game plan. I'll have to bring some of the lures up here."

"Whatever you need to do. Just get 'em out of here. I don't want Bobby having anything to do with them anymore."

"They're not dangerous, Steve, just annoying. Basically, I relocate them to someplace where they can be themselves without wrecking anyone's yard. They seem to like it in their new home. I'm even getting kind of fond of the little guys. Pixies...now, that's another story...vicious little things—fae equivalent of the mosquito but super-sized. We could do without. Tanji's working on designing some pixie wards to keep them away once we've cleared up an infestation."

"Just handle the gnomes, Ron." Steve went back into the apartment and closed the door.

Ron waved to Bobby, who was watching from the window, but then Bobby's father pulled the curtains shut quickly as the boy started to wave back.

"Huh, wonder what put a bee in his bonnet..." Ron squatted down to get a look at the lean-to burrow and smiled at one of the gnomes who peeked out at him from beneath it, "So...what are we gonna do with you?"

The gnome bared his teeth, and then pulled his head back into the mass of cardboard. Ron could hear all of the gnomes speaking at once, but he didn't understand much gnomish yet despite Tanji's efforts to teach him. No matter what they were talking about, the gnomes were nowhere near a garden, so it should be easy to lure them into the truck and transport them to their new home.

He backed the truck up into the loading zone at the bottom of the stairway and lifted the back sliding door. Securely fastened at the front of the truck box interior was a five-foot-tall ceramic gnome with a full huddle of live gnomes he'd collected earlier in the day gathered at its base. A few of the eight gnomes turned to look at him when the door opened, but they quickly turned back to their newfound god once they'd identified him. Ron knew he didn't have to worry about any of them taking off if he left the door open. His experience with gnomes to this point showed them to be extremely predictable when in the presence of their new deity.

He grabbed a box full of smaller ceramic gnomes from the back of the truck and started up the stairs. As he went, he set them down in a path that led up to the back of the truck. He set the final one right in front of the cardboard burrow and gave a whistle to get the living gnomes' attention.

The same gnome who'd popped his head out of the makeshift burrow before poked his head out again. He blew a raspberry at the ceramic gnome and disappeared. Ron raised an eyebrow. *Well, there's something new.*

Suddenly, all four gnomes came barreling out of the

burrow. Ron was cheered by this—back to predictable gnome behavior, except...*gloriosky! That's not supposed to happen.*

The gnomes joined together to lift the ceramic gnome and loft it up and over the side of the railing. Ron heard it shatter as it hit the hard sidewalk below. The gnomes ran to the next one and repeated their actions. Ron started running then, hoping to outpace them and grab up the rest of the lures before the vandals got to them.

He was not going to enjoy explaining to Steve Moore that the gnomes appeared to be set on staying.

This Magic Moment

T HOMAS SET A TRAY of brownies on the coffee table and slid them across to where James sat reading. "Try these. A bit of a different recipe than the last batch. Baking is nearly as demanding as magic."

"What, did you forget the chocolate?"

"Oh no, you'll find plenty of chocolate...I merely added a few things that increase the health factor."

"If you added sprouts, just tell me now, so I can prepare myself for the shock."

Thomas answered in his normal, measured tone, "No sprouts, mate."

James took a big bite of his brownie and looked thoughtful for a moment. "Can't quite place that little extra taste. I'll have to have some more," he said as he took another bite. "Yeah, I may just have to eat all of it."

James finished the brownie quickly and grabbed another.

"Not going to be whinging on about them not being up to snuff, then?" asked Thomas.

James shook his head, his mouth too full of brownie to answer, and returned to his book.

"Brilliant," said Thomas, as he stood up and walked nonchalantly behind James and calmly leaned down to whisper in his ear.

Thomas caught James as he slid into unconsciousness and slumped forward, his head sinking toward the hard, wood coffee table. He pulled James's body back to lay limply against the chair with his head lolling off to the side. Thomas carefully dragged the chair over to the window and turned it so that James was facing outward to the street.

He opened the window and took a spray bottle from his pocket, soaking the front of James's shirt with its contents before he spritzed some of it onto the window sill. The odorant fulfilled its purpose. Although it was nearing midnight, Thomas could see the wisps that clustered near the building begin to gather just beyond the sill in the light from the open window.

Thomas walked behind James, placed his hands on the sides of his unconscious mentor's head, and began to chant.

＊〜＊〜＊

Lizbet's mom called out from the kitchen as Lizbet came through the door, "How was Bobby? Is he behaving for his father?"

"I don't know, Mom. I didn't really get to see him," Lizbet replied, walking into the kitchen and setting her backpack on the kitchen table.

"No? I thought you were riding over to your dad's after school."

"I did..." Lizbet was quiet for a moment, then she said, "...but dad said I'm not allowed around Bobby anymore."

Her mother spun around quickly and looked at her daughter questioningly, "What? What do you mean he said you can't be around him?"

"Just like I said. I kind of learned how to use my wings today...and Dad says I can't be around Bobby until I stop using magic. And I don't know how to do that, because I'd lose these wings in a heartbeat if I could."

Lizbet yielded to her mother's hug, "I know you would, sweetheart. I know how much you wish things could go back to normal for you. And I'm so sorry that your father said that. He and I have always disagreed on a lot of things, but we've seldom disagreed about what's best for you kids. So there's a first time for everything. He's not going to keep you from seeing Bobby. He can't. Bobby lives with us, not with him."

"I don't want you guys to get in a fight about this. I mean, you've been getting along so well lately, and you already have enough stress..."

"Honey, I don't care if you have wings or horns or two heads. Your father isn't going to keep you from seeing your brother. The world has changed, and he's going to have to adapt to that, at least where his children are concerned. I also am not going to let him fill Bobby's head with any anti-fae nonsense. He and I are going to need to have a conversation about all of this when I pick Bobby up tomorrow evening. Until then...just remember that your father has been known to say some stupid things, but he loves you. That I know for sure. He'll come around."

Lizbet walked to the kitchen and rummaged for something to eat, deciding on an apple and hot chocolate. After she pulled the steaming hot water out of the microwave and dumped the packet of chocolate and one extra teaspoon of sugar into it, she sat down at the kitchen table.

"The thing is, I was feeling really rested today, and I didn't have a headache at all. I was feeling good for the first time in a long time and then, wham! Dad makes me feel like I've done something terrible." Lizbet stirred her cup of chocolate vigorously. "I mean, I know it was maybe dumb to offer to take Bobby flying, but you said you thought he was feeling left out, and I just wanted him to know that I hadn't forgotten about him."

"I think that's sweet, Lizzie. Although offering to take him flying may have been a little over the top. We'd have to discuss that. And it would have to be not too far off of the ground...what am I saying? It's so difficult to believe that you can fly!"

"Yep, it was pretty amazing."

"I can imagine. I wish I could! It would save me a lot of complaining about the traffic."

Lizbet laughed. "Well, I'm not great at it. It kinda took me by surprise."

Mom sat down next to her and patted her hand. "I'll talk to your father about this. And I'll win. Until then, just stay out of his way. You'll see Bobby tomorrow night, and maybe by then you can show us both how well you fly."

Tanji smacked her father's hand as he tried to sneak a spoonful of the stew she was stirring on the stove. "You can wait until Mom gets home! She's only home from New York a couple days per week and you can't wait for her?"

"You're more like her every day. You certainly are quick on the draw...let me run something by you about gnomes."

"Sure, go for it..."

"Today, I tried to remove a huddle of gnomes and they didn't respond to the ceramic lures. In fact, the gnomes destroyed as many of them as they could. What do you think of that?"

"That's plenty weird. As far as I know, fae gnomes have worshipped garden gnomes since people first started making them. Before that, their gods were pieces of driftwood or stones that had a gnomish form. They have a *big* worship thing—they always build their burrows around objects that represent gods to them. Was there already anything there that they could be worshipping instead?"

"Not that I know of. They're also not dug in for this burrow. They've built one out of cardboard on the second floor of Steve Moore's apartment complex."

"Lizbet's dad?"

"The same. He has Bobby staying over there, and the gnomes are camped out on his doorstep."

"You know, Lizbet told me that the gnomes put the statues at her mom's house in the trash. I guess I didn't think about how weird that is. I'm going to have to find out more. I was just getting ready to do that blog for you about gnomes and their beliefs, and now maybe I don't know as much about it as I thought."

"Yeah, well...Steve wasn't real pleased when I told him that his gnomes weren't responding to the usual lures and that I'd have to come up with something else. So, if you find anything out that I can use, let me know right away. The last thing I need is for this new business to fail because I can't manage what I've said I'm going to do...but the good news is, the Johnson's huddle went right for their new god and are merrily burping away out by the cabin."

"It's a good thing Gramps doesn't use that broken down

cabin anymore because he moved to Florida and turned the land over to you."

"I'll say. I'm thinking about turning the cabin into a pixie house. What do you think?"

"I think you better make sure my pixie wards work first. No way are you going to want your work following you home when you're dealing with pixies. I also think you're going to need something more than wards. Fortunately, I found an entire chapter in Langoureth's book about how to keep them from breeding."

Thomas continued chanting, and as he did, a faint blue light extended from his hands and surrounded James's body. At the window, one of the wisps slowly drew closer and closer to James's still form. Then, responding to what was now an irresistible attraction, the wisp rushed toward and into James's chest, disappearing. The faint blue light brightened and the aura around James's body hummed for just a moment, then quieted.

Another wisp followed. Then another, and another, and another.

Thomas opened his eyes as the light surrounding James become piercingly bright. He smiled and removed his hands from their places at James's temples, watching as the aura slowly faded and then disappeared.

He could hardly wait until James woke up and felt the magic flowing within him again. They would truly be mentor and student then, with James in possession of not only Myrddin's knowledge but also the bright pulse of magic.

~~*

It took a moment for James to orient himself when he woke up. He was sleeping on the flat's one living room chair in front of the open window. He didn't remember having turned the chair away from the coffee table. He felt woozy for a moment and...*wow, I feel fantastic, strong.*

And then, Myrddin's memories kicked in, and he understood why. He was feeling the tingle of magic. Where had it come from?

He stood up, turned around, and saw Thomas was sitting on the couch, observing him with an intense expression.

"What just happened?"

"You feel it, don't you?"

"And again...what just happened?"

"The wisps. You've soaked up some of the wisps."

"Tom, how did I soak up the wisps? Did you do something?"

"I was sure you wouldn't mind when you felt again how brilliant it is...isn't it fantastic, having the magic there?"

"Tom, I said no when you asked me if I wanted magic. You *know* I don't want this. I don't know how you managed it—you've obviously learned lessons I didn't teach you, but you need to undo it."

Thomas looked at James for a long moment before he said, "I can't. The wisps are bonded. They're part of you now, as much as Myrddin is."

James's mouth clenched up small in suppressed anger, and he could feel the back of his neck beginning to burn with the heat of it. Without speaking, he walked past Thomas, out of the door, and into the night.

CHAPTER EIGHT
Are You Taking This All Down?

J AMES WALKED THROUGH THE brightly lit early morning streets of London, alone for the first time since Fae Day. No wisps followed him. Myrddin was no longer without his magic, and the wisps no longer sensed him as being incomplete.

James thought about what it meant for him. He hadn't wanted the magic because he knew if he'd had it when Thomas kidnapped him in Scotland, he would have brought down vengeance on his head and probably killed him outright. Myrddin had been the most powerful sorcerer of his age, perhaps of all ages. James was afraid of what having that kind of power would mean.

In Myrddin's time, he and Morgan had used their powers to heal, to protect their Kingdom, and to work to unite the humans and the fae in a peaceful relationship for their mutual interest. While James was interested in all of those things, he didn't think he had Myrddin's patience or wisdom. He was more likely to take action based on the way that he felt in the moment, and he was pretty sure that impulsivity could have dire circumstances when it was backed by Myrddin's powers. Myrddin had elven magic. His natural talent was for the magic of war even though he had fought his nature and mastered the magic of peace.

James wanted to sit, to think, to be silent, but the rush of magic inside him made him restless, so he walked on. He hadn't felt the energy of magic so intensely when he was Myrddin, he felt sure of that—what had Thomas done to him? How much magic had Thomas given him?

He was furious with Thomas, but why had he expected anything different? Perhaps the elves understood better than he had the persistence of personality throughout lives. He had begun to realize over the past month that Thomas directed all of his behavior toward only one end, and in this newest incarnation, that end was toward the support of the fae and their magic despite being hated by all of them. The fae live a long time and keep their history close. No matter what Thomas did for their sake, the fae were not likely to forgive him.

James had taken Thomas's education on instead of returning home after Fae Day. He'd done it to prevent Thomas being used by his brother monks for his new magic. He'd committed himself to Thomas for Myrddin, to see that Faolan's magic was not abused in this lifetime and to give Thomas a second chance to get things right. Had he failed? Or was Thomas simply not capable of seeing anything beyond his own worldview? Although Thomas had ignored James's wishes, he hadn't placed James in danger, and he was sure that Thomas truly believed he'd given him a valuable gift.

James sighed. It wasn't easy being a parent. What could he do but take Thomas back to Ohio as planned and hope that he could somehow teach him to temper his thinking to see other points of view?

The fae struggled to wake Lizbet's sleeping body. Lizbet had begun to fight back with more stamina, even though she was unaware of her nightly struggles. The girl had won the battle the night before, and Morgan had been unable to travel within the aether to her court in Europe as she had planned. Tonight, she was sure she would push through the girl's resistance again. Her spirit had been weakened by her father's harsh words.

Pushing hard, she managed to shove the girl's consciousness back into the space that contained the memories of her past lives. She would now be available but inactive like the memories of the human Morgan, the unfortunate Maude, and the six other lives whose memories had been delivered to Lizbet with the amulet she must always wear around her neck. Morgan was in charge again.

Morgan had tried to remove the amulet to rid herself of Lizbet, but she had been unable to do it. She didn't understand how this could be. Only Morgan could remove the amulets she had made, and when she did, the memories of all of the wearer's lives would disappear. This is how Lizbet had destroyed Faolan at the base of the Tree of Life. Removing the amulet would remove Lizbet's memories and the memories of her past lives, leaving Lizbet's young body for the fae half of Morgan to claim as her own.

Still, the amulet had not yielded to her. It would yield if Lizbet tried to remove it, as it had when she had cut away

Faolan's: how could Lizbet have this power if she did not also have it? How could Lizbet be more of the original Morgan than she was? The amulet should have recognized her. It was absurd to think that this child, Lizbet, was more like the first Morgan than she was.

Still, it would be a shame to destroy her—Morgan admired her courage and would have let her be if not for Myrddin. She might even have shared her magic, her rule, but she could never share her one great love. While she sometimes felt the stirrings of compassion, she quickly tamped them down.

No, there was no other choice. She would force Lizbet to live among her whisperers where she would be of no consequence. She dressed in one of the long gowns she had compelled Lizbet to buy and then faded into the aether. Lizbet was a silly girl to think that taking control of the ability to fly was close to the full power of her magic. Morgan had abandoned that ability long ago for anything more than a short trip. She preferred a quicker route.

Tanji woke suddenly as the ward she'd set before she went to bed sent a pulse of alarm through her body. *Gotcha*, she thought, *who knew such a powerful fae could be so predictable?*

Tanji moved quickly to perch on the edge of her bed, fully dressed. Across from her, the fae who wore Lizbet like a costume was illuminated in the pale blue light cast by the magical net that surrounded her. She stood with the ancient book on the dresser open to a page of spells, and her eyes moved along the page hungrily.

Morgan nonchalantly turned away from what she was reading and said, "Oh hey, Tanj, your dad let me in...I would have asked first if I'd known you had a ward around the book…"

"Really? I mean, really? You think I can't tell the difference between some hagged out old fae and my awesome BFF? Have you forgotten how well Langoureth knows you? Have you forgotten she promised to prevent you from abusing your power?"

The fae's expression quickly changed to a snarl. "And how will you stop me, little girl? Langoureth may be with you, but *you* are not her. You do not have her power."

"And you don't have Morgan's power, or you would have won your battle with my friend already. You won't win."

"You know so little. I always win."

"Not this time. Not here. And not against my friend. You can't even get the book you're here to take. Funny, isn't it? The great Queen Morgan trapped in a simple ward that was conjured by a half-fae."

"Are you prepared to keep me here forever, then? Your ward won't help you when you have to release me."

Tanji waved her hand and the fine, blue netting woven from light disappeared. "You're free now. As long as you don't try to touch what's mine again. By the way, if you try to harm me in any way so that you can take the book, the book will sense it and burst into flame. One that can't be extinguished until every bit of it has been consumed," said Tanji, grinning at the fae, "We were always evenly matched in power, Morgan, just not in ambition. You're right, I'm not Langoureth. Unlike Langoureth, I won't run from you. Harm my friend and learn exactly what *I* am capable of."

"You'll cede the book to me soon enough. I can wait," Morgan said as she faded from the room.

Tanji stood up and walked to the closet door, opening it as she took deep breaths, finally able to admit to herself that her heart had been beating so hard she was sure the neighbors could hear it. She nearly squeaked when she said, "She's gone."

Eamon walked out of the dark closet and looked up at her in the gloom, "You did well, lass. I knew you wouldn't need the backup. And now we have the measure of her—she doesn't have her full strength or that ward would never have held her."

~~*

James sat across from Thomas, and for the first time, he wished that he was able to channel more of Myrddin. He wanted to be the elderly druid with beard, sandals, and robe for this conversation. It would lend more gravity to his words than his 19 year old mug, hairless chin, and pleasant, geek-guy appearance could possibly convey.

"I've spent the morning thinking long and hard on this, Thomas. I considered leaving you here and returning home alone. I feel betrayed. You discounted everything I told you and did what you wanted to do instead of respecting me." James paused, gathering his thoughts, then continued, "You don't owe me anything. I know that. I stayed here with you free of all expectations. But before today, I believed that I'd earned your respect. It's upsetting to learn I haven't."

"But I did it because of my respect for you..."

"You did it because you wanted to impose what you believe on me."

"No..."

James searched his mind for what Myrddin would say. "Be silent, Thomas. If you respect me, you'll listen."

"As you say," Thomas replied, echoing the formal language of the elves he so hoped to be united with.

"I've told you about Faolan…that he was Myrddin's grandson, that he murdered Myrddin and bound the fae. I've told you that Lizbet, Eamon, and I captured you, and Lizbet destroyed your amulet and memories so that she could free the fae. But I haven't told you why I stayed with you instead of returning home with Lizbet."

Thomas nodded and remained silent.

"I haven't told you because I thought it would hurt you to understand how much you are despised. But Thomas… you *are* despised. Without me, the elves would have killed you as soon as they found you. I wanted to give you the opportunity to finally live a life free of the influence of all of your past lives. But you seem determined to take the same path by dedicating yourself to a cause and not hearing anything that doesn't fit with what you believe. If you live your life like that again, I'm afraid it will have a disastrous outcome. You can't help but have the magic, but you also can't continue to pursue the attention of the fae."

James stopped talking, and Thomas looked at him expectantly.

"Go. You can talk now," said James.

"I meant no disrespect, James. You're my only mate. I just wanted to share my joy with you. I've never had a friend, at least, not one that I remember. I guess I don't know how to be a friend. I'm sorry."

"Being sorry is a start, if you mean it and aren't just saying what you think you should say. Paying attention to what I just said is critical. Do you understand that you're in danger from the fae if you continue the course you're on? And that you endanger everyone around you?"

"I don't understand that, no. The fae respect Myrddin because of his great mastery of magic, and he was only partially fae. Why can't they grow to respect me, too, and allow me to join them?"

"Thomas, you're not even half-fae. When the realms split, your magic existed as a wisp—a lost, soul-less thing that the fae abhorred. They would have destroyed them all if they could. Humans who have magic through rejoining with a wisp are on the fae most-hated list. And although most of the other fae accept them, elves hate all mixed blood humans. But even the accepting fae don't feel the same about the wisp-joined. None of the fae want anything to do with them. And now you've turned me into one of them."

"But you're Myrddin. They won't turn against you."

"They will if they learn how I got my magic. You better hope they don't, because Myrddin and I are all that stand between you and death. And again, Thomas, you need to hear me...if you continue along this path, you risk every-thing, including the respect the fae have for Myrddin. I've extended you my protection. If you continue to behave in ways the fae wouldn't accept, they'll start to question my judgment. If they decide I've extended my protection unwisely, they'll come for you, and they may also come for me. That's not an outcome I can get behind, so are you listening? If you can't agree to look for interests outside of this single-minded obsession with impressing the fae, I'll leave you here when I go home. You'll be on your own, then, without Myrddin's protection."

"No, James, I don't want that. I can try, if you show me how. But I can't give up the magic."

"I haven't asked you to. I just want you to realize that you need to be human as well as fae—have interests, make friends, read a book or watch a movie once in a while. Playing a fracking video game! I understand now that I did this wrong when I started in training your abilities right away. That was Myrddin, the teacher side of me, kicking in. I should have started with just helping you to be a guy. Because I, James, am really good at just being a guy."

"Well, then I guess I could use some lessons in being a guy. How do I start?"

James held a hand up, palm out, "A high five would be a good first step."

CHAPTER NINE
You Make Me Feel Brand New

L IZBET WAS FEELING DOWN when she first woke up, but she broke into a wide grin when the phone on her nightstand vibrated, signaling the arrival of a text from James.

"we r @ heathrow. flt out soon. cle-hopkns @ 9:30 pm"

She quickly texted back.

"do u want 2 b picked up"

"can u?"

"chking w/ tanj"

Lizbet fired off a text to Tanji asking if she would be

available to pick James up that evening and got the response she was hoping for.

"we cn get u - send flt #"

She realized she hadn't asked her mother if it would be okay to go. She ran down to the kitchen, fearing she would take off flying as she went down the stairs. She was so light, so happy, even though she felt like she had barely slept.

She grabbed her mother, who was making a stack of pancakes for breakfast, and gave her a big hug. "James is coming home tonight! Can I go with Tanji to pick him up? Say yes, say yes, say yes!"

Lizbet's mother smiled, "It's been a while since I've seen you this happy, kiddo. So, okay, I'm saying yes."

"Woohoo!"

"But...and this is a big 'but', you've only just turned 16 and James is 19. And, let's not forget a little something about a trip to Scotland he involved himself in without mentioning to your mother where the two of you would be. So...I need to get to know James better before you two start running around town together. You can pick him up, but then you come straight home. Understand?"

"Yes! You are the best mother in the world."

Lizbet continued to beam as she ate her breakfast. There was no way she was going to be able to focus at school. James was coming home. Having him back where she could hold his hand wouldn't fix everything, but she was confident it couldn't make things worse.

~~*

Lizbet racked her bike and locked it up. Behind her, from the loose group of boys loitering on the school steps, she heard catcalling, and then one of them called out, "Nice rack."

She chuckled to herself. Tanji sure knows her jerks.

As she walked up the steps, Tanji came clattering up the stairs behind her and fell into step with her as she entered the school hallway. "Are you so excited you can barely stand it? Your geeky hottie is coming home!"

"Like I need to be reminded! I don't know how I'm going to stay focused in school today. This morning over breakfast, I was trying to review everything I studied last night for Physics, and I kept blanking out, grinning to myself like a big goober and thinking about James instead."

Tanji opened her eyes wide and nodded her head with big, exaggerated movements, "I'm sure that will go away once he's here. Focusing on school will be much easier."

"Yeah, yeah, yeah. I don't care. I'm walking on clouds today. I can hardly wait to see him."

"Don't forget, Langoureth gets to see her brother again for the first time in over a thousand years, so I'm a little excited myself now that James and I are kind of related. I've been Little Miss Envy for years because you get to have a cool brother. So, maybe I've got me one now, too."

"I hadn't thought about that. It's weird, but what isn't anymore?"

Tanji put on a more serious face and said, "'But chica, it's not just James arriving on that plane tonight..." as Lizbet opened her locker and chucked in some books she didn't need until after lunch, "...how do you feel about James bringing company?"

"You had to mention that when I was trying so hard to forget it. It's going to be uncomfortable, what else? I have all these conflicting memories and thoughts about him—a lot of them from Morgan, but some of them mine. At one point a month ago, he was stalking me, James, and Eamon around Scotland, probably completely willing to kill all of us, so it's hard for me to see Thomas as someone safe, no matter what James says about him. James actually *likes* him even though he's the reincarnation of the guy who murdered Myrddin...and the whole 'he's my grandson' factor is more than a little weird, too. My ancient Morgan has all these memories of him as this sweet-faced, serious little boy that she adored."

The crowd in the hall was rapidly thinning, so they did their quick BFF hug and took off in opposite directions down the hall to class. As they parted, Tanji said, "I need to talk to you about something soon, but I want to wait until after you can think about something other than James, so be ready for a big, serious talk tomorrow."

Lizbet nodded, not really registering her friend's serious expression. She almost passed right by the door to her classroom, distracted by the happy cloud of bliss that surrounded her. It was a strong day. No headache. Lizbet had faith now that whatever had been hurting her since Fae Day was going to be easier to handle with James around. They'd already been through so much together, and he always had her back.

Lizbet lingered at the coach's office door after PE class. Since she was feeling confident and strong that day, she might as well say to Mrs. Armstrong what she'd wanted to say to her the first day of school.

"Moore, you waiting for me for a reason?" the teacher said as she passed Lizbet in the hall and continued in to her office. She tossed volleyball into a large wire container as she walked past it on the way to her desk, "If you are, better take a seat."

Lizbet followed her into the office but stood next to the chair instead of sitting. This kept her at eye level with the woman who was eyeballing her back while sitting on the edge of her sturdy metal desk. "I just wanted to tell you that it isn't right I can't run with the team. I didn't grow an extra set of legs or get super strength. I've just got wings—useless ones, too. Mostly, they just get in the way. They are definitely not going to make me a better athlete. There's no reason I shouldn't be allowed on the team."

Lizbet kept eye contact with Mrs. Armstrong. The teacher's tough expression softened a little as she did.

"Moore, I didn't make the rule. I didn't even say I like the rule. I've got a nephew in California who never learned how to swim, but since Fae Day he dives right in at the beach and stays under water for hours at a time. The gills and fins he grows when he hits the water really help. So, I get it. But I also wouldn't let him compete on the swim team. It wouldn't be fair to the other kids."

"That's kind of different, isn't it?"

"I don't know. Can you really say for sure that there's nothing about you that won't affect your running abilities, even things you don't know about yet? According to my sister, Jared keeps finding out new things about himself every day."

"No, I can't say for sure...but I'm really going to miss being on the team."

The teacher looked thoughtful for a moment. "Okay, kid...here's what I can do. No one said you couldn't work out with us. You can compete with us during practice and be water girl at the meets. Would that help?"

"Mrs. Armstrong, thank you! That would help. I wish

I could participate all the way, but being able to compete during practice will be great, if that's the only way I can be on the team."

"Sure—it'll probably help a couple of your team-mates if they've got somebody else at their level to go up against. Might even give us a stronger team. And if anyone on the school board has a problem with it, I don't think they're going to be able to come up with any good reason you can't participate as a non-competitor."

As Lizbet walked to her next class, she not only felt like she'd won a worthwhile victory, she felt pretty grown-up about it. Two days ago, she'd gone off like a scolded puppy with its tail tucked between its legs when the coach told her she couldn't be on the team. Today, she'd faced down what had been hurting her, and she realized her coach probably hadn't even meant to make her feel bad. She thought that if she could get back that level of confidence all the time, things would definitely be a few more steps toward normal. Even the headaches seemed to stay away when she was acting like the old Lizbet, the wingless Lizbet.

"Hey runt," Lizbet called out when she heard Bobby's voice as he entered from the garage with Mom.

"Hey Lizzie-tizzie," her brother called back.

Lizbet walked over to hug him as he entered the kitchen, and he pulled back just the slightest before he stopped himself, smiled, put his arms around her neck, and hugged her tight.

"Dad says I can't go flying with you, so don't try to make me."

"I wasn't thinking of taking off right this minute anyway."

Lizbet got him in a gentle headlock and rubbed the top of his head with her knuckles. "How about noogies? Are noogies okay?"

Bobby shouted, "Stop, stop! Mom! Make her stop," but he was laughing, and Lizbet loved hearing it. Maybe things really were going to go back to normal.

She let her brother go, and he bounced over to the sliding glass door to the backyard, then turned back to her, "Hey, the gnomes are all coming back now, too. I'm glad, because Daddy wanted to have Mr. Ross take them away. I wouldn't like it if anybody hurt the gnomes. That just wouldn't be right." Then he was out the door, laughing, as a group of gnomes ran up to him, begging him to play.

As she watched her children roughhouse, Sheila realized that this could be any day like it had been before Fae Day. Inside her, something relaxed that had been full of fear for too long. Lizbet was acting like her old self, and Bobby seemed none the worse for wear after two days listening to his father's anti-fae talk.

Steve had tried to convince her that Bobby shouldn't be exposed to Lizbet until Lizbet gave up magic. Sheila wasn't having it. She'd bundled up Bobby's things and then sent him to the car, telling him she'd be out in just a minute. She watched him all the way there, making sure that he was safe as he crossed the small parking lot, and then she let Steve have it.

"Don't ever, and I mean *ever* talk about our daughter that way around our son. Lizbet didn't choose to be half-fae, and although I don't like that she lied to us to help the fae, what she did to save them was brave and honorable. She has more guts and strength of conviction than anyone I know. And don't try to convince the little boy who worships her that she is anything less than a fantastic big sister, do you understand me?"

"Sheila, magic is dangerous. You've seen it yourself."

"I haven't seen anything of the kind. The gnomes aren't any more dangerous to have in the garden than the deer or the rabbits or the neighbor's cats. They're just not as appealing visually as the wildlife. But Bobby has fun with them, and I have never once seen them be too rough with him. If anything, they seem to be keeping an eye on him to protect him."

"Yeah? What about pixies? And ghouls? And dragons? What about them?"

"You could also say a lot of negative things about coyotes, bears, and rats, but I don't hear you telling your son to stay away from your daughter because she's a mammal."

"Sheila..."

"No, Steve. I have just one last thing to say....I know you love your son. I also know you love your daughter. If you want to lose both of them, then keep going the way you're going. But if you want to keep them, then you need to take a very close look at the way you've been behaving. I would never tell your children to avoid you, you know that, but your kids...they're smart. They'll pay attention to what you do and say and make up their own minds about you. You better make sure you're not telling them you can't accept them for who they are."

〜〜*

"Again this week, lass? I'm quite the popular laddie," Eamon said as Tanji made her way toward him up the hill where he stood watch over the herd.

"Maybe you could try coming into town once in a while."

"Perhaps. Perhaps. But I'm retired, remember? Does no one remember what that means? It's about time people started asking my opinion as a wise elder instead of tellin' me what to do like I'm still a lackey. No, I don't mind a bit staying out here in the wild and having you come to me...anyway, I've saved a nice seat." Eamon waved a hand toward a flat rock a few feet away. "Make yourself at home."

"Eamon, I don't think of you as a lackey. I think of you the way Lizbet thinks of you—as a friend. I told Lizbet she should come by to see you, by the way. Did she?"

"As it happens, we did run into each other. Didn't she mention it?"

"No, she was upset about her father when I saw her. He said he doesn't want her near Bobby anymore."

"I know about that. I was watchin' her at the time. I kept myself hidden because her father isn't all that fond of me."

"He's not fond of anything magical, I guess. He hired my father to get rid of the Moore's gnomes. Did you know that one of them followed Bobby to school and attacked a boy? They also built a burrow out of cardboard at Mr. Moore's apartment. Bobby was staying there for a few days, and a bunch of them followed him. They're acting weird."

"I do have to say, that concerns me. I noted they were present on the walkway—it's not a smell I could miss—but I didn't know they'd gone to ground there, so to speak. Gnomes follow gods, not little boys. Has there been any other unusual behavior where Bobby is concerned?"

"No, they're just following him. Oh...they did throw away all the ceramic gnomes from the Moore's garden one day. And they broke the ones my father tried to use to lure them into his truck. Does that mean anything?"

"Och, the gnomes aren't ones for breaking up gods. I need to think on this, maybe do a little observin'. To speak plainly, the real problem with the gnomes is that they're stupid. And to my way of thinkin', magic and stupid is quite a bad combination."

"Well, I really just stopped by to ask you if you wanted to come to the airport with me and Lizzie to pick up James and Thomas."

"Is James home tonight, then? Och, and Thomas...I still don't trust that one. A nasty piece of work he was...in that case, magic and *smart* were also quite a bad combination. But no...I've work to do in the Moore's garden now. But thank you for lettin' me know. I'll want to be keeping a sharp eye out on that Thomas as well. I think James is far too innocent to understand what that one is about."

CHAPTER TEN
Battle of Wills

THE FEEL OF MAGIC was extraordinarily strong whenever James was next to him, but, as Thomas walked through the terminal, he began to feel another powerful presence and an only slightly weaker one beside it.

Langoureth's magic was a diffuse, swirling aura around and through Tanji. The magic in Lizbet had a much different feel—encapsulated, guarded, and concentrated into a hard essence that had very little interaction with the girl except for a hot flow into the girl's back where a set of wings lifted away from her shoulders. No—this fae had not integrated with her human half. Morgan contained herself within, not sharing or investing her human vessel with any of her power. Interesting.

Thomas felt the magic that was hidden from the girl flare

up like a lighthouse beacon warning of the rocks below as he saw Lizbet's eyes alight on James.

~~*

Lizbet said, "There they are!" as she pointed toward James and Thomas coming through the security gates toward the baggage claims area.

"Wow, girl, that's your grandson? Mmm…girl, he's fine."

"Tanji! Look, I told you about him. Really—not a good idea."

"A girl can look. Just sayin'."

Lizbet didn't respond because James had rushed to her and swept her up in a giant hug. Her feet were off the ground and she hugged him back fiercely. She didn't think about anything else until he finally let go and set her down, snagging her hand in his as he released her.

"I don't think you and Tanji have ever met officially, but…"

James looked closely at Tanji then, and let go of Lizbet's hand to reach out and take both of Tanji's hands in his. "Langoureth…"

"Myrddin…it's been so very long a time."

Lizbet felt a little left out then, as the memories of brother and sister connected through her friends. After a while, James broke the moment and said, "Tanji, this is Thomas, your great-nephew, I suppose. It's nuts how we can be strangers and yet be family at the same time, right?"

Tanji and Thomas exchanged greetings. Thomas's greeting was dutiful; Tanji's was enthusiastic and flirtatious. Lizbet really didn't like how obviously interested in Thomas Tanji seemed to be. She also hadn't been as prepared to see him as she'd hoped. His gaze kept returning to her in an expectant way, a friendly way, but she still wasn't sure she could ever feel anything about him other than mistrust and anger.

~~*

Eamon concentrated on the glamour and then walked into the Moore's backyard from the woods. He hoped the gnomes weren't feeling overly ambitious so that they'd try to go after a large deer instead of their usual smaller dinner fare. Of course, if they did, he wasn't likely to fall for their trap. Gnomes are small: their magic is limited. Like all fae, it's adapted to the needs of their bodies and their culture. Gnome magic is almost entirely utilized for trapping food and protecting themselves from enemies.

Eamon, like most people, found the final outcome of gnome magic sickening. They can create an invisible barrier that allows some materials to pass through but stops other materials cold. When they hunt, half of the huddle runs after the unfortunate animal, shouting and waving sticks to chase them in the desired direction. The other half waits, hands joined, chanting their spell. The barrier stops the hide, the bones, the teeth, the brain, and the guts on one side but allows the meat to travel through. If the animal stops moving, the gnomes behind provide a push to get them through. Their prey is dead and skinned before it knows what hits it. Effective but less than tidy.

Eamon manipulated the appearance of the glamour to give an impression of grazing but kept his eyes and ears active as he watched Bobby and the gnomes playing in the dusk. Sheila Moore appeared at the back window to look in Bobby's direction every so often and would then disappear from view again. He assumed she'd satisfied herself that Bobby was in no danger.

Eamon, on the other hand, was confused by the absence of ceramic garden gnomes around the burrow. He looked the area over carefully and didn't see anything else that could have taken their place as the gnome's object of worship.

When Sheila called Bobby into the house with "Bobby, time to come in. It's too dark now," Bobby started for the door and the entire huddle followed after him. What Eamon heard them calling the boy as they babbled along behind him alarmed him. The wee laddie appeared to be safe for now, but there was every chance that, with time, he'd find himself in danger.

After stopping at the front of the house briefly to let his landlord know he was home, James led Thomas up the steps to his over-the-garage apartment. It was exactly as he'd left it when he'd made an unexpected detour to Scotland a little over a month before. He did a quick zoom around to pick up articles of clothing he'd dropped here and there and hadn't picked up after, quickly disposing of them in the bedroom hamper.

Thomas was still standing outside on the landing with the suitcases, waiting for instructions, when James walked back into the main room.

"Sheesh, Thomas, come in! Mi casa es su casa!" James said, walking to pick up a suitcase and haul it into the apartment. "It's small, but it's home. I've got a nice air mattress I use when I'm camping, and it should be comfortable for you to sleep on. We can store it in my room during the day so that we aren't constantly falling over it."

Thomas walked to the back of the room where the refrigerator, stove and sink served as a kitchenette. He opened some of the cabinet doors and looked inside. "It's good to see you have a decent amount of storage space in the kitchen." He walked to the door and then walked back with one of his bags. He opened it and began taking out jars and boxes.

"Thomas, seriously, we don't need to get everything unpacked tonight. I thought we could just chill, get a pizza, watch some TV, and have a little housewarming celebration."

"I'd feel more comfortable if I can make sure nothing was broken or spilled on the plane, and you know I feel more at ease when I'm organized."

"Yeah, yeah...let me help." James walked to the narrow closet that was crammed in between the fridge and the wall. Inside, it had four shelves, mostly empty. "I can probably give up this whole cabinet, since the only thing I keep in here is my SCA gear, and I doubt I'll need it anymore, so it can go in the top of my bedroom closet. Who's going to let Merlin play at being a knight in a Renaissance Faire? No, I think they'd want to put me on show in a whole different way."

James pulled his rattan sword, his shield, maille shirt, and armor out of the cabinet and reached far into the back to grab for his helmet. As he snagged it and turned around to place it in the pile of gear, Thomas almost smirked and asked him, "So, you were a medieval knight before you were a sorcerer?"

"It's a group I'm in. We re-enact medieval times. It's kind of a geeky thing to do, so maybe don't mention it to Lizbet? I think Eamon knows about it, but she doesn't need to know that I was fantasizing about being her knight in shining armor the whole time we were traveling across Scotland. Like she needed one!"

"Your secret's safe with me, chum. Although it could be worse—you could have turned out to have been playing at being a monk for several lifetimes." Thomas smiled at his own joke.

James held out his hand for a high-five and Thomas returned it, "You're really starting to get the hang of this just-be-a-guy thing, Tom. Wait until I introduce you to a little thing called the TV remote—you'll never be the same again."

The girl was fighting her again, strengthened by the time she'd spent with Myrddin's arm around her in the back seat of Tanji's car, caught up in each other for the hour's ride from the airport. Morgan had attempted to insert herself in their goodnight kiss, but Lizbet hadn't yielded even a moment of her experience for Morgan to share.

It was a small victory for the girl, and Morgan let her have it without causing her pain. There wouldn't be many more victories for her. Morgan's plans were already in place.

Except for the day when the gnomes had pulled her out of hiding with their constant shrill voices, Morgan had stayed well hidden during the day and taken her freedom only at night. Even that served to weaken the girl's resolve. Humans are so dependent on things like sleep, food, friends, and family.

Morgan had lived as a full fae for fifteen hundred years now. Among the fae who have near immortal life-spans, many things lose their importance over time. She could live without sleep, without food. She had long forgotten her mortal father, the closeness of the tie she had once forged with Langoureth, and her love for her fae mother who had yielded herself to the aether eight hundred years ago rather than to continue to live her life in the shadow realm.

What she'd not forgotten was the feel of his hand in hers, the joy she felt in his arms, the power of his touch to soothe her. She was a nymph: she loved with great passion, and she could not forget the only man who had ever made her feel that love. It was the most important thing for any nymph to be forever with her one soul-mate once she found him. Now here he was, returned, and she would have him.

Shortly after Lizbet closed her eyes to sleep, Morgan banished her easily to the back of her own mind. Morgan quickly dressed herself in the prettiest of her gowns. With James so close, she didn't need to ride the aether tonight. She slipped out the window and floated to the apartment above the garage next door. She looked in eagerly at the first window, hoping to catch a glimpse of her sleeping lover. Instead, Thomas sat there, looking out the open window and smiling at her as if he'd been expecting her. He reached his hands out to her above the sill with his palms open as though to take her hands in his. When she realized his intention, Morgan abruptly phased into the aether, reappearing on a hill several miles away.

"Tell me what you know about this human they call Thomas!" she shouted, fuming, at the short figure standing beside her.

"Och, good evening to you too, mistress. It's been a while."

"Tell me, Eamon. What do you know about this Thomas?"

"Precious little, if truth be told. He has no memory of

his past lives now, as you should recall, and he knows only what James has told him about his experiences and previous lives. He'd know your relationship to him all those years ago. He has natural magic with the same gifts he had when he was Faolan, I would expect." Eamon reached a hand up to seat his cap more firmly on his head. "And do you remember, you told me I could retire?"

"You're a gruagach. You're bound to me and to my house forever. You'll always come when I call."

"As you say, mistress. I will. Why do you need this information about Thomas, then?"

"I went to look for Myrddin, but it was Thomas I found, and he seemed to be waiting for me."

"Well...Faolan had a talent for sensing magic even though he kept his own hidden from the kirk. He had a way of knowing where a creature was and what it was doing. It's how he tracked your Myrddin on the trail at Dunipace so easily.

"But why would he greet me with open palms, ready to take my hands? He tried to destroy the fae. T'was all I could do not to pull the air from his body and strike him from the face of the earth."

"That wouldn't be the wisest choice, if you're trying to pass as young Lizbet. I think I'd recommend against it. Plus...that James, I've heard he has great plans for the lad. I think he'd miss him, so you might not want to go rockin' that boat if you don't have to. Anyway, Thomas has no interest in harming the fae. Not in this life."

Morgan felt strange, then. Woozy, a sensation she could never remember having. Fae don't get light-headed. And yet she was. How very strange. It was even stranger when she lost consciousness.

～～*

Lizbet was disoriented. As she opened her eyes, she felt damp grass beneath her, and she looked up to see the moon and stars above instead of the ceiling of her room.

"Mistress?" someone said, and then Eamon was bending over her, "What's happened? Are you alright, then?"

"Eamon? Where am I? And how did I get here? Why aren't I at home in my room?"

"Och...Lizbet, now that's quite a good question...sleep flyin', do ye think?"

"What? Really?" Lizbet sat up, looked down at the gown she was wearing, and back up at the gruagach. "And sleep dressing, too? Last thing I remember, I was in bed in my pajamas and thinking happy thoughts about having James home."

"I'd say it's quite a mystery, then. I heard a bit of a noise, and there you were. Why don't we get you home, and you can worry about how all of this happened tomorrow."

Lizbet looked down at the gruagach whose golden eyes were wide with innocence, an expression she recognized well as the face he wore whenever he was holding something back from her. He knew more than he was saying, but she also knew he wasn't going to tell,. It was more than infuriating.

Whatever. He did that sometimes, and it usually all worked out for the best. She didn't have to like it, but she trusted him with her life, and while he often did things his own way, he had never done anything that would hurt her. She started walking, and the gruagach fell in beside her.

CHAPTER ELEVEN

Can't Get You Out Of My Head

TANJI OPENED THE CAR door and leaned in, moving to set her purse on the passenger's seat when she saw that Eamon was already there, his small feet up on the dashboard, neatly folded at the ankles, stretched out with the seat reclined, his hands behind his outsized head as a pillow. He was snoring quietly.

"Little dude, what are you doing in here?"

Eamon woke and was immediately focused. "I need to chat with you, lassie. There are all manner of strange things happening with Lizbet and her brother."

"Okay, but talk while I drive, 'cause I can't be late for school today. I have a massive French test."

"Okay, right...so, yesterday, the fae Morgan was standin' there talking to me when she collapsed all of a sudden. When she woke up, it was Lizbet lyin' there in the field with no memory of how she'd gotten there. I couldn't say anything because Morgan would hear, and I don't want her to know that I've been serving two mistresses."

"Well...what did Lizbet think happened?"

"I might have suggested sleep-flyin' as a possible explanation."

"Really? I'm sure she went right along with that."

"It was the only thing that came to mind. She may even have been confused enough to believe it."

"None of this sounds right to me. How is it that Lizzie hasn't got a clue the fae is taking her over and running around with her body without her knowledge?"

"I don't know, lass, but I can't be the one to clue her in... if Morgan knows that I'm watchin' out for the lass, I'll have no way of knowing anything from now on. If she thinks she can trust me, I'll still have an eye on her and be able to report back if I find something that can help Lizbet. But you'll have to keep from her what I've told you."

"Yeah, well...guess it's me who has to break through all that denial. But she just isn't listening."

"Then you've got to find a way to make her listen. She's fighting back in there, I'm sure of it. It's how she pushed the fae out last night, not even aware of it, and ended up in that field, but she needs to figure out how to take control all the time. I get the heebie-jeebies thinking about what Morgan has been doin' flyin' around with the young lass's body every night."

"Don't even go there..." Tanji shuddered.

"And that Thomas...he knew Morgan was coming, he was waitin' for her to visit next door."

"What does Thomas have to do with it?"

"Morgan told me she'd flown to the window next door in hopes of catching a glimpse of Myrddin, but what she found instead was Thomas waitin' there as though he'd been expecting her. She also said he seemed mighty glad to see her."

"Seriously? Well, I could keep an eye on him, 'cause I don't mind." Tanji smiled.

"You're not thinking about Thomas as a romantic partner are you? I don't think that's a good idea, lass. I don't trust him."

"James seems to, and he's been with him for the past month."

"I haven't talked to James about him yet, but I'm telling you to be wary. In every life I've known him, he's sneaky and more than clever about getting his way without anyone knowin' what he's done. I don't need to be worrying about you as well as Lizbet."

"You want me to keep an eye on him or not? I'll put on my big girl pants and try to control myself," Tanji said as she pulled the car into the school parking lot and waved to a group of friends as she drove by them. "You know, it doesn't really help my reputation to be driving around with a gruagach riding shotgun. Most people get your kind confused with gnomes."

"Aye, that's because, like gnomes, those people also have brains the size of walnuts."

Tanji laughed as she maneuvered the car into a parking lot. "I knew that would get you. You need to learn to chill, little dude."

"And as to the gnomes...the Moore family gnomes don't need ceramics anymore. They've adopted Bobby as their god; I heard them saying it, and that definitely will not be good for the lad. They have a tendency to make sure their gods never go too far from the burrow. While they followed him last time, I worry about what might happen if they decide he shouldn't be doing that kind of travelin'."

"You know, I heard them saying 'king' about him when he stopped Morgan from hurting the gnomes, and it didn't occur to me that what they were really saying was 'god', since it's the same word for both in gnomish. I thought they were just talking about playing king of the hill. Could it really be a problem?"

"Aye, it could. So, I'll not be spending quite so much time with the herd. Bobby and I are about to become even better acquainted."

~~*

Lizbet had been tired all day from her midnight walkabout, but when she woke up on a bench in the locker room after school, she was sure she hadn't been so tired that she'd just fallen asleep. She looked at her watch, and it was too late for track practice now, even though she was dressed out for it. The girls would be re-entering the locker room soon. *What in the world is going on?*

As the team made their way back inside, the coach called out to her, "Moore, my office. Now."

Lizbet walked into the coach's office, and coach closed the door behind her. "What were you thinking out there?"

"Huh?"

"Don't. Just don't...you said you wanted to be able to compete, and then you grab the baton and fly it to the next runner? I thought you were serious about wanting to be a part of the team, but I guess you really pulled wool over on me this time. You disrupted my practice with that stunt, and I won't have my practices disrupted."

"But...I didn't even make it to practice, coach. I fell asleep in the locker room and didn't wake up until the team came back in."

"So you're telling me it was the other team member with wings who flew your leg of the race? You had your chance. You blew it. You're off the team, Moore. Don't come around looking for sympathy again, I'm not buying it next time."

Lizbet stood up, fighting the urge to cry. The last thing she remembered before track practice was leaving her Physics class and turning down the hall toward the gym, and then she'd woken up face down on a bench. That was it. That was all she remembered. A big chunk of time was missing, and she had no idea where it had gone.

She went back to the locker room and changed out of her gear, packing it all up in her backpack because she wouldn't need to keep anything in a locker anymore. The rest of the girls had already taken off, and she was alone. She let one tear slide down her cheek before she dried her eyes on her shirtsleeve and headed into the empty hall. She was never going to be normal again if she didn't start facing what she'd been denying—she hadn't been alone in her body for a long time, but she now knew for certain there was one extra version of Morgan in there who had no interest in playing nice.

When she got to the front of school to get her bike, she'd never been so glad to see Tanji sitting out front in her car, waiting. The trunk popped open, and Tanji called out the open window, "Stow the bike, girl. You and I need to talk."

* ～ * ～ *

"So...I know you don't want to hear this, but girl...you're living one mucked-up life. Jenna sent me a video of you flying around the track. What is going on?"

"Well, it isn't sleep-flying like Eamon was dumb enough

to suggest to me the other day...Tanji, I finally have to admit it, I think you've been right all along—I've got a fae inside me who wants to wreck my life. And I was ignoring it because I was trying so hard to pretend that everything would just go back to normal. Like I *could* be normal after everything that's happened. Maybe the wings should have tipped me off, right?"

"Hey, they say admitting you've got a problem is the first step to recovery. So, where do we find a 12 Step Fae-Possessed Anonymous Program? This is exactly what we needed to have a serious talk about. Because I had a visit from Morgan two nights ago, and she tried to convince me she was you. She tried to get her hands on my spell book."

"Why didn't you tell me that right away? Not that I could have done anything about it, I guess. I think the best person to talk to would be James. Not James exactly, but Myrddin's memories. He might know something that could help."

"Yeah? But he didn't get the magic with his memories, did he?"

"No, he didn't, but he still knows more about magic than any of us. Langoureth and Morgan mostly know about healing, but Myrddin...he didn't focus on just that aspect. He explored all kinds of magic. Maybe he knows something that can get this fae out of me because none of my past-life ladies are coming up with anything."

"It's worth a try." Tanji turned her head to look out the back window as she backed out of the spot, "I hope he's got some food. And I hope that dishy Thomas is there."

"Tanji...don't even think about it."

"Okay, I'll keep my hands out of the cookie jar. I

promise." Tanji made a serious face but she could only hold it for a few seconds before she broke out in a grin.

James opened the door when Lizbet knocked. He smiled and leaned into her for a hug, which she happily returned, basking in the contact. If only she could just stand here forever. James said, "I wasn't expecting you."

"Yep. I wasn't expecting to stop by, either. I would have called, but it's kind of...well, stuff is happening, and I can't deal. I need your help. Or really, Myrddin's help." Lizbet shot a quick look over James's shoulder to where Thomas sat, grinding herbs in a blue ceramic mortar at the tiny kitchen table.

"Come on, enough of the hugs, big bro, we can't stand out here all night!" Tanji giggled behind her.

Lizbet looked at Thomas again, and said, "James, maybe we could take a walk. It's...personal. And I'm sure Tanji would love to talk healing and herbs with Thomas, if he's okay with it."

Thomas nodded, "I'm replacing some of the potions I had to leave behind in England. I'm always happy to talk magic."

Tanji slid past Lizbet and walked into the apartment toward the kitchen, "You got anything for keeping pixies away? I tried my hand at a ward, but it only lasted for an hour or two and then, wham! We had pixie city all over again. My dad really needs something more effective. You don't want those things around your pets or your kids. They have a really nasty bite."

Thomas's expression brightened. "I might have just the thing." He picked up a notebook, flipped through it, put it down, and then picked up another. "Yes. This might do. I wonder if I have all of the ingredients..." He walked a few feet to the small kitchen and motioned Tanji toward the full length cabinet, "...forage in there for fennel, if you could. And is there a jar of beetle parts?"

James and Lizbet were still standing in the doorway, but Lizbet tugged gently at his hand as she started walking down the stairs. "I think we can probably leave the kids alone without them getting into too much trouble."

James followed Lizbet down the stairs, his fingers woven together with hers as they held hands. They walked in silence to Lizbet's front yard where they sat down on the garden swing that overlooked the flower beds. Lizbet pulled her feet up and sat cross-legged while James rocked the swing gently, his long legs firmly planted on the ground.

Lizbet seemed hesitant to begin. "So...here's the thing. You know how everybody expected me to have Morgan's magic and memories, and that never really happened except for these freaking wings?"

"Yeah, but I didn't think you cared about the magic that much."

"I don't. I don't care at all, but the problem is...I think the reason I didn't get the magic and the memories is because Morgan is in there trying to get rid of me." Lizbet paused, shook her head slowly from side to side, and began talking again. "You know how I've been having horrible headaches and was tired all the time for like a month? Well, now I'm losing time, and I've woken up sometimes in weird places with people telling me that I was doing stuff I don't remember. And I can fly—I did once, at least—which tells me that there's magic hanging around in there, and maybe I've even been flying a lot more than I know."

James nodded, thoughtful. "Let me ask you this...do you own a long, blue velvet dress? Kind of matches your wings?"

"Yeah, why do you ask?"

"Oh man...and how about a red satiny one with a gold belt?"

"Yeah, that one, too."

"Then you've doing some major flying—like transatlantic flights." James looked thoughtful for a moment and took both of her hands. "I thought I was dreaming, but maybe I wasn't. Maybe Morgan was coming to visit me and hanging around just outside my bedroom window. I saw you there a couple of times as I woke up, but...I thought I was still asleep and dreaming about you because I missed you."

"So, she was, like, just hanging there, watching you sleep?"

"Yeah."

"Wow. How creepy is that?"

"Major creepy, now that I realize it wasn't a dream." James stopped rocking the swing abruptly. "You know, she must be in there right now, creepin' on every word we say. I've gotten used to Myrddin hanging around, but his memories are all background stuff these days. He does feel like a part of me now..."

"Good. Because I want Myrddin to really apply himself to figuring out how to get Morgan out of me. I don't want her in there. It's just too bad you don't have all of Myrddin's magic. 'Cause then you could put a whammy on her." Lizbet scrunched up her forehead and sighed. "Headache time again. What do you want to bet Morgan isn't too happy right now?"

"Yeah, about the magic...this seems like the right time to tell you something. Something I haven't told you yet, because I was still trying to work out what it means for me..." James paused briefly and then continued, "...I do have Myrddin's magic again, well...not his, but as good as. And maybe even more magic than he had, because I don't know how many wisps Thomas shoved in there."

"Huh?" Lizbet sat up straighter and cocked her head, punctuating the question.

"Thomas re-magiced me. Knocked me out to do it. I'm still not sure what kind of spell he worked, but he's promised he won't do it again to anyone. But...yeah, I've got a lot of powerful magic flowing through my veins. And it worries me, because I don't have the kind of patience and restraint that Myrddin had. I could impulsively blow someone's head off with a lightning bolt if they looked at me the wrong way."

"Hardly! You're not exactly a hot-head."

"Maybe not as much as when I was younger and had to work so hard to control it, but when we had Thomas in that van after he kidnapped me, I *really* enjoyed taking him down and tying him up. If I'd had magic then, who knows what I might have done to him. Magic is as much an act of will and focus as any chant or potion. And I was willing serious pain on him at that moment."

"Yeah, you also could have beaten him senseless when he was tied up...but you didn't do that, either. Because it's not you. I really don't think you have to worry."

James's face softened and his voice quieted, "What I worry about is that someone will hurt *you*, and I'll just lash out. It scares me. Do you understand?"

"I do. I feel the same way about you. I'd fly up overhead and drop bombs on anyone who tried to hurt you!"

"Bombs, huh?" James asked, teasing her.

"Well, my sandals might fall off and hit them in the head or something." Lizbet smiled.

He returned her smile. "Yeah, more likely....look, because Morgan's hanging around in there, I don't want to talk anymore about how we get her out. But I'll confer with the old man's memories once he and I are alone. And I'll figure something out, even if I have to get medieval on that fae. I hope she's listening and knows Myrddin is on to her and fully stoked up with magic, because she's not going to mess with you and get away with it."

"We better go check on Tanji and Thomas," Lizbet said, standing up, "I still don't like him, but I guess I'm going to have to get used to the idea of having him next door. I'm also pretty sure you're going to be seeing a lot of Tanji with him around." Lizbet stood up and rubbed at her temples. "And I think Morgan heard you loud and clear, because my head is pounding like a disco."

CHAPTER TWELVE
Splinter In The Soul

J AMES SET CERAMIC GNOMES out in a line from the truck to the back yard of a split level house with a nicely landscaped yard. At least, he suspected it had been a nicely landscaped yard before the gnomes got to it. Their burrow holes were everywhere. He called to Mr. Ross to take a look at an especially large hole.

"With all of these holes, there have got to be at least 20 gnomes living here. Do we have enough room left in the truck?"

"I think so, but it's going to be a tight fit. It's been a good day for the service, that's for sure."

"Do you think we should tell people the cabbage they're growing is responsible for the young gnomes?"

"The cabbage?"

"You know how people tell their kids they found them under a cabbage leaf?"

"Yeah?"

"Gnomes really do find their kids under a cabbage leaf. Cabbage has some kind of weird role in making baby gnomes. Don't ask me how it works…"

"How do you know that?"

James bowed, laughing. "World's most powerful sorcerer at your disposal, but keep that on the down low. I just wear the dirty coveralls as a disguise."

"I forgot the part about you being a sorcerer. You're Langoureth's brother's half-fae, right?"

"Sort of—close to the same concept, but Myrddin and I were brought together in a slightly different way than the half-fae were."

"Tanji told me that she was getting a brother. It surprised her mother and I, that's for sure! I'd forgotten it was you." Ron looked thoughtful, remembering, "Then again, in those first few days after Fae Day, just about everything overwhelmed me. But we're doing great now. Tanji seems to really enjoy her new abilities, and I like that we can work together on fae-related projects. I'm planning to open a shop with her. Sell potions and wards, that kind of thing. Who knows? Maybe someday we could make it a franchise. I just worry she doesn't have time to make everything she'd need to stock a store like that, even if it was only open a few hours a week."

"My room-mate Thomas could work for you. He's good at the healing arts, and I can vouch for him being a fast learner. He and Tanji really seemed to hit it off, too."

"Can he work in the states? He's a Brit, right?"

"I think that if the job requires having magical training, Thomas is one of the few people in Ohio who would qualify for the position. If you were willing to sponsor him, it could work. That way, he can stay here longer. I worry about him being on his own with such a limited life history."

"You know, James, I don't mind at all you being my girl's surprise brother. You definitely know how to help her out, and it's nice that you're looking out for you friend." Ron nodded toward one of the burrow holes, where a young gnome popped his head out. The gnome caught sight of the statues. "I think we've got a bite!"

Soon, there were five or six gnomes standing on the lip of the burrow, talking animatedly about the large gods that had shown up while they were inside. As the first group started walking along the line of gnomes to investigate, a few more appeared from another hole and then quickly followed their huddle-mates.

As the duo followed the loose group of gnomes back to the truck, where they were struck silent by the sight of the 6 foot tall gnome, Ron said, "What about you? Wouldn't you rather work in a warm, cozy shop than slog around in the weather chasing after gnomes and pixies?"

"No, I wouldn't. I like the job so far, and you're paying me well, so I can't complain. Plus, I may have magic, but I haven't decided yet if I ever want to use it. For the past week, I've been focused on not accidentally magicing my way through things. It would be easy for me given how adept Myrddin was. I'm just not sure doing the easy thing is always the best thing," replied James, "...plus, the more you depend on magic, the more likely you'll run up against unintended consequences. As a short guy I know is fond of saying, 'magic can be tricksy'."

"I can respect that. Okay, Thomas it is, if he'll have the job and the work permit can be worked out...and assuming Tanji clears him as an employee."

James grinned. "I don't think Tanji will have a problem with it."

"Good lookin' guy is he?"

"So I understand."

James shooed gnomes out of the way as he carefully closed the back doors of the truck with the gnomes inside. When he was done, he waited for Ron to return from collecting the fee from the homeowner. As Ron returned, the homeowner went into the garage and walked back out with a shovel, heading for the back yard.

Ron smiled as he walked past James, "That cabbage tip was really appreciated. Want to stick around for some coleslaw?"

Thomas stirred the clear, red liquid, and then lifted the spoon out of the pot to let the contents drip off the edge. It wasn't thickening as quickly as he would have liked. He wondered if he'd let the solids steep long enough before he strained them out. He waved his hand over the pot, and spoke a few soft words. The liquid flared blue for just the briefest moment and then returned to its original red. He wished he could stop worrying so much—it was coming along just fine. He simply couldn't stop being a perfectionist, even when brewing the ingredients for a healing tea. What Thomas did best was focus.

When the mixture thickened to the right consistency, Thomas carefully poured it off into a small glass jar and stoppered it with a cork over which he spoke a sealing spell to assure an airtight seal. He then placed it in the refrigerator, next to a growing collection of brightly colored potions. At this point, he and James were covered for several years for the symptoms of just about any illness: warts, vomiting, poor eyesight, pixie bite, even the vapors.

Thomas had only been practicing magic for a month, but already he was bored and ready for greater challenges: he wanted to begin to learn a more involved magic—the kind James had but wouldn't use or the kind he felt next door whenever Lizbet was home.

He treasured the moment two nights ago when her magic had burst from the tight kernel where it was hidden, possessed the girl's body completely, and Morgan floated toward the house where he had been sitting up late reading. He'd gone to the window to wait for her to pass. She came to the window, but when she saw him, her face darkened and she retreated to the aether instead of taking the hands he reached out to her in friendship.

He understood she must have come for Myrddin as she had in London—he'd sensed her there many times, just outside James's window. Was a dead romance all she was interested in? It seemed ridiculous, unthinkable, that such a powerful fae, the queen of his kind, would be focused to that extent on rekindling romantic fires with a wisp-endowed human. And yet, if Morgan could be so attached to one of the wisp-endowed and see him as an equal to stand beside her, couldn't she and the other fae come to view Thomas as one of their own over time?

Thomas was cheered by this. All of his work so far had been toward that very goal. He knew that James was holding back on him with much of Myrddin's knowledge: the most powerful wizard of his time would not have restricted his magic to healing spells and protective wards. He'd have known magic to make the universe sing for its power and its beauty. If James was going to hold out, then perhaps Morgan would teach him.

He would wait every night, hoping that the next time she would take his hands.

* ~ * ~ *

Lizbet looked in the mirror, trying to see behind her own questioning blue eyes to the woman who hid there in the background, waiting to take over when Lizbet dropped her guard. Lizbet had stayed up all night watching videos on her tablet, struggling to keep her eyes open. She didn't want to lose that feeling she had after James kissed her goodnight to waking up in a strange place with no memory of how she'd gotten there.

"You can just bug off, Morgan! You're not taking off with my body again if I can help it. So just let go and get your butt back into the background where joined faes belong!"

Although she knew she looked like a total loser chewing out her own reflection, she felt a lot better afterward. She was going to need some caffeine, but she felt good enough to make it through the day even without sleep. She figured she could take a nap in afternoon study hall, and Tanj could keep an eye on her to make sure that Morgan didn't possess her and get her into any more trouble.

She knew she was going to have to tell her mother about what was happening, and she wasn't sure that her mom could handle one more bad thing this week. First, there was Bobby's problem at school, then she was kicked off the track team for good, and to top it off, the gnomes were becoming even more annoying. They were constantly waiting for Bobby just outside the patio door, instead of staying in the garden doing their gnome thing. At least her mom had never grown cabbage, so the small huddle of gnomes wasn't growing in size.

She tried to remember how she knew about the cabbage connection to gnome-babies. It certainly wasn't one of her own memories. And then she remembered—Myrddin had taken Morgan into the fortress garden to show her the new-born gnome under the cabbage leaf. It had been adorable and so very tiny, and you forgive babies for unseemly bodily noises. Myrddin had pulled her quickly away when he saw the adult gnomes coming to claim the child. He cautioned that the only time gnomes became truly dangerous to humans or other fae was when they were protecting their themselves, their children or their gods.

She walked down to the kitchen and slid into her seat where her mother had a bowl at the ready and the cereal lined up. Bobby had snagged the sugary stuff and was keeping it close, but she was more than okay with healthier choices. She was an athlete, after all. And then she realized she wasn't an athlete anymore, so she might as well indulge herself.

"Bobby, pass me the Sugar Crumb, wouldja?"

"Don't take all of it," he said as he shoved it toward her.

"What if I do?"

"I'll sic Gurrdenn on you!"

Mom walked quickly to the table from out of the kitchen, hands on her hips, eyes squeezed into slits, "Young man, after everything that's happened this week, you think that's a funny thing to say?"

"I..."

"No. You can go up to your room and stay there until I say you can come out. I know that you wouldn't do what you just said, but I don't even want to hear you joking about it. People will believe you."

Bobby made as much fuss and noise as he could on the way up the stairs without actually doing anything that could get him in more trouble. Lizbet hid her smirk about how obvious he was being.

"And you can stop smirking, young lady!" her mother said.

"Sorry, Mom."

Her mother sat down at the table across from her and sighed, "I was too harsh, wasn't I?"

Lizbet gave a small shrug, "Maybe just a little? The poor kid is just being a dork, same as always."

"Oh, I know. I guess I just didn't realize how other people were going to react to our having a half-fae in the family or how upsetting their reaction would be."

"Well, I'm glad that you accept me for how I am, mom. And I know that Bobby appreciates it, too. He wouldn't want anything bad to happen to his gnome buddies. He was major upset when Dad wanted to get rid of them. I explained that Tanji's father would never hurt them, so I think he felt better about it, but I don't think he gets why people get so upset about gnomes."

"No, I expect he doesn't. Children are generally very tolerant unless someone is telling them to be otherwise. I'll let him come back down in a few minutes. I'm not sending him to school without breakfast."

"Mom...I do have something I want to talk to you about, and I hope it doesn't freak you out."

Mom raised her eyebrows, "Oh lordy, what now?"

"Ummm...you know how I've been having headaches and have done some things that are out of character for me? Things maybe you've seen and wondered about?"

"I agree you've been irritable lately. Yelling at your brother, just general meanness sometimes. I assumed it was because you were worn out from the headaches."

"Umm...except that I would never yell at Bobby. Tease

him, noogie him, and call him a name or two that I don't really mean; yeah, I'd do that. But actually yell at him? No, and as far as I know, I haven't. The poor kid. No wonder he was feeling so left out. I need to explain this to him..."

"Could you explain it to me, first?"

"Okay, so...you know how on Fae Day, when people who became halfers got their new memories and abilities and it was all just pretty comfortable with the new fae side sort of accepting that they weren't going to be in charge? Well, it didn't happen that way for me. My fae never settled in—she's in there, separate, hanging out just waiting for a chance to grab control. And apparently she's been taking over a lot, especially when I'm asleep. James says he saw her in England."

"How...?"

"Don't know. But remember how everybody expected me to have really strong magic because Morgan was a powerful fae? Well, she's still got all of that magical power, and she's not sharing. I don't really know how she's doing it because, unlike Tanji with Langoureth or me with the human Morgan, I don't have the fae Morgan's memories to draw on."

Her mother's face softened in concern, "How can I help you, sweetie?"

"If I do something that you think isn't like me, tell Tanji or James. They may be able to help if they know when Morgan is taking over."

"I can do that. If I think it's Morgan I'm interacting with, should I say something to her?"

"No. You should stay away from her. She might be dangerous. I don't know. And...she's probably in there listening, too. I don't really have any secrets from her. But I will. I'll find a way to do something about her sneaking around in there all the time. I have to. She isn't going to win."

"I don't understand any of this, honey, and I'm just frazzled trying to get all of this right for you and Bobby, I think you know that. But keep talking to me about it. I don't want you to feel that you have to keep things hushed up so that they don't upset me...but I'm not sure that you should share this with your father."

"Oh, no way! I don't even feel like talking to him right now..."

"Just remember—he loves you, but he isn't always right."

"I'll get over it, but I just can't really work on that relationship right now, you know what I mean?"

Mom nodded. "I do. Now, go on...the last thing I need is to hear that you've been late to school because we were sitting at the kitchen table jawing."

James watched the pirate bobble-head on the dashboard bobbing up and down as he relaxed in the passenger seat of the gnome removal truck while Mr. Ross drove them to their next stop. This one was for the business's first pixie removal. The job would be more difficult than working with the gnomes. A lot more could go wrong.

They pulled the pixie cage out of the back of the truck so they could get to it easily when they captured the pixies. They also pulled out the nets they'd brought and got dressed in matching sets of heavy denim coveralls, gloves, helmets, and face masks.

Pixies have a nasty bite, and their dust can have both hallucinatory and stimulant effects if inhaled or ingested in too large a dose. They had jars and hand vacuums to gather any dust that had collected below the pixie nest. They hoped to take some back for Tanji because it could be useful for magic in the right hands.

They quickly found the nest in the corner of the customer's old barn. James recalled his first pixie hunt as a boy. He hadn't been quite so well dressed for it, and he had come home covered in bites but bursting with feelings of success about the number of pixies he and his friends had captured and released several miles away. They'd left wards so that the pixies wouldn't try to return to their nest once the boys were gone. *Wait, those are Myrddin's memories,* James thought. *Wow. I'm not even trying to keep them separated anymore. I guess that's what I get for spending so much time digging around in them so that I can do a good job with Thomas's education.*

He watched as Ron approached the largest pixie, a whopper at around 6 inches tall. He swung the net, and the pixie easily avoided it. It made a run at James then, baring teeth that were normally hidden in a deceptively sweet-looking face. James ducked as the pixie dive-bombed him, and then he tossed up his net, capturing it easily. *Thanks to Myrddin, looks like I've got some muscle memory for this.*

Ron thumped him on the back after they'd managed to capture and cage all five of the pixies. "Nice work!"

"As it turns out, I've done this before," he said as he took off his thick gloves and shoved them into his back pocket. "What kind of wards are you putting up to keep the pixies from returning?"

"Tanji made a couple of wards last night that look kind of like...what do they call them? Dreamcatchers. She's sure they'll work better than her last run at it. They have something in the thread that pixies avoid."

"Fennel based?"

"I couldn't tell you. The magic talk makes me go all deer-in-the-headlights. But Tanji says it's the bees knees for pixie warding, so I'm going with it. She made them so that they look decorative, too. Apparently, pixie wards are going to be all the rage soon. We'll sell a million of them."

"I had no idea there was so much financial potential in the fae," James laughed, as he lifted his side of the cage and they started for the truck.

"Young fella, this is the U S of A— there's financial potential in anything if you can figure out how to monetize it. I did that for other people for twenty years. I think I like this better. I get to make my own hours, provide people with what they need to deal with a changed world, *and* I get to help people understand new ways of looking at things to boot," replied Ron. As they loaded the pixies into the back of the truck, he continued, "I do have a vested interest in trying to make a world where people like my daughter—and like you and Lizbet, too, I guess—get a fair shake even though you're a little bit different."

Chapter Thirteen
Am I Awake?

THOMAS WATCHED THE WISPS at the edge of the small pond. Some would assume they were morning mist and not even notice them, but Thomas could feel the pull of their magic. Ever since he'd healed James, he'd begun to think about other ways he could harvest the magic of the wisps for the good of the Fae. He'd used the wisps' natural attraction to James along with a magical pheromone to draw them. He wondered if the pheromone on its own would be enough to draw the wisps into a host and if he could increase his own magic in the same way.

Thomas took off his sandals and waded into the pond. The mud was cool and soothing between his toes. He was there to gather the starweed that grew in the shallow water at the pond's edge. The plant had once been known for its ability to absorb background magic, and if the wisps had been lingering around the pond long enough, the plants may have soaked up enough of it to make a source powder for light-casting. Not that light-casting was all that valuable in a world where everyone carried a phone with a flashlight in their pocket, but it still might have a use, and the powder would keep forever if it was properly stored.

After gathering the starweed and stowing it in a large plastic bag, he explored the shore of the pond for other valuable plants, but he didn't find anything of interest. Although Ohio was certainly better for collecting herbs and wild plants than London, he was still impatient because it would take so long to find and gather the things he couldn't purchase.

James had told him about the opportunity to work in the Ross's magic shop with Tanji. He wasn't interested in sharing magic with the non-fae, but it would certainly provide an opportunity to increase the range of his magical explorations. It might also bring him into contact with other half-fae who were seeking tools for their magic.

Thomas thought Tanji was frivolous. He also found the obvious interest she'd taken in him unsettling. He had no knowledge of females in the slightly-over-one-month span of his memory, and he didn't know how he was supposed to respond to her teasing and flirting. Although he had no memory of being a monk, he also had no memory of interacting with women. He could remember the details of all kinds of practical things—he was able to cook simple, healthy meals without a cookbook, and he'd repaired several small items in the flat in London without having to consult a manual. He had a legacy knowledge of the London Underground James often said he envied. But girls? His mind was blank. He had no idea how he should behave.

What he didn't need memories to know was that Tanji, with her huge brown eyes, long ringlets, and generous mouth was a very attractive girl—what any normal, healthy, non-monk his age would call "well fit". Yes…well fit, indeed.

Lizbet had slept a total of six hours in three days. She'd gotten most of the sleep when Tanji was there to fend off Morgan if she took over. So far no problem. But she didn't know how much longer she could keep it up. She had dozed off sitting up in English class, although she'd jerked awake quickly, disoriented, when her forehead hit the desk. That was lots of fun. A hot blush had spread quickly across her cheeks when the kids started laughing.

She had been sure that having James back would make the difference in her life, but it had lit just a brief bright spot and now she was exhausted, in danger of her grades taking a real nosedive, and frightened of what Morgan would do if she let her guard down for even a minute. It was only a matter of time before she had to sleep or her mother noticed and forced her to get some sack time. She tried to focus again on what her history teacher was lecturing about, but her attention wandered…

She woke up on the floor with the school nurse kneeling above her, waving smelling salts under her nose.

"Lizbet, how do you feel?" the nurse asked as she helped Lizbet sit up. She took her wrist and checked Lizbet's pulse against her wristwatch as she talked.

"I'm okay. No problem."

"You fainted and fell out of your chair. Have you taken anything that could cause that? Any medication or other substances?"

"No…I…I haven't been sleeping much."

"Can you get back into your seat for me, or do you need help?" the nurse asked.

"I'm good," she replied as she got up and sat down in her chair again. The boy in the seat behind her looked up, snickered, and then settled back down to his reading as the nurse slipped a blood pressure cuff around her arm and shushed when she objected.

When the nurse undid the cuff, she said, "Your blood pressure is normal. I don't think you fainted."

"No...I think I probably fell asleep. I'm very tired."

"I'm taking you to the infirmary and we'll talk about this there. Can you make it under your own steam?"

Lizbet nodded and stood up, following the nurse out into the hall while trying not to hear the quiet laughter behind her.

James was surprised when Lizbet's mom called him and asked if he could pick Lizbet up at school. He was even more surprised by the reason. When Lizbet had fallen asleep on his shoulder watching TV in the Moore's living room the night before, he didn't think anything of it. She'd slept for about an hour and woke up as the show ended. It worried him that she had been intentionally staying awake.

James signed in at the front desk, and the front desk administrator pointed him in the direction of the nurse's office. When he got there, Lizbet was sitting in a plastic chair in the nurse's waiting room. She yawned as he approached, although she tried to hide it.

"Your mother is really upset that she couldn't pick you up herself. When she told me *why* you were waiting to be picked up, I got upset, too. What were you thinking?

People have to sleep, Lizzie." He turned and walked briskly toward the front of the school.

Lizbet stood and trailed him as he turned to walk back out to the parking lot.

"I was thinking I didn't want to do any more sleep-flying. You know why. Who knows what my body has been running around doing while I was asleep? It freaks me out."

James slowed his pace so that she could catch up. He realized that he shouldn't be angry with her; Lizbet wasn't the one who was responsible for the problem. "Yeah, I do understand, but I don't think that's a good way to go about it. You know that Tanji and I are both working on this, and we'll figure something out. We will. If you need people to keep you safe until we do, you need to talk to us." James put his arm around her then, realizing how alone she must feel to not have reached out to her friends.

"Tanji, your mom, me...we'll all do everything we can to help. Thomas would help you, too, if you'd let him."

"Yeah, because I am *so* ready to be Thomas's good buddy."

"Look, you were there and you already know this: Thomas is *not* Faolan. In fact, what he believes is completely opposite to what Faolan believed. He really has had a new start in this life, and it would help me out if you acknowledged that and got to know him as he is."

"Really? You want to have this conversation now? When I'm so tired I can't put one foot in front of the other?"

"Yeah, sorry. It's just that he asks about you every day. He has this idea that you're something special, and it would mean a lot to him if you could accept him." James opened the car door for her, and she curled up on the seat, laying the side of her head against the backrest. James said, "Seatbelt."

"Are you my mom or what?"

"Yes. I've been deputized as mom until I get you home

and you are in your bed getting at least eight hours of sleep. And I mean it. Your mom is depending on me to keep you in line, and I'm going to score some big points with her by doing exactly that, even if it means I'm missing work in my first week at the new job."

"I can handle you getting points so we can leave the house together sooner. Go ahead and mother me."

Lizbet dozed off before James pulled into the driveway of the Moore's house. He hated to wake her up to get her into the house, but he didn't want to have to sit in the car while she slept. Lizbet was five foot nothin' and looked perfectly comfortable, but even with the seat all the way back, his six foot frame was too tall to allow him to rest comfortably in the car. He walked around to open the passenger door and leaned in to shake her gently, "Okay, sleeping beauty, your carriage has come to a halt. Time to go to the ball."

Lizbet rolled over and sleepily said, "You've mixed up your fairy tales. Sleeping beauty gets a kiss."

James kissed her lightly on the forehead and smiled. "Don't distract me when I'm being your mom."

"Ewww...the image I just got about that is more than disturbing," Lizbet said as she got out of the car, "Wishing I was unconscious again..."

James walked with Lizbet up to her room, where she slipped off her shoes and got into bed fully clothed.

"I'm going to be downstairs, so if you wake up and need anything, just call. Your mom asked me to stay and check on you every so often to make sure that you really are sleeping, and Mr. Ross was cool about giving me the rest of the day off in exchange for working part of Saturday on a pixie removal, so I'm going to pop over to my place and grab a book, but then I'll be right back."

"Sure, whatever…" Lizbet managed before she rolled over onto her other side and fell asleep.

Freoric peered out from behind a tree in the park where Thomas waded through the pond gathering weeds. He found his assignment distasteful. No elf would be pleased to be in a place where the humans swarmed like pixies, and he longed to return to France to be among his own kind. However, the Elders had tasked him to follow the monk, and follow him he would, no matter how he despised the job.

If it were left to him, Freoric would put an arrow through the abomination's heart and end him. He couldn't understand why the Elders were holding off on the inevitable.

Over the past few days, he'd managed to keep an eye on Thomas without being spotted by him or his protector. The Elders still held Myrddin in some regard, but Freoric had seen no evidence that Myrddin's current incarnation controlled Myrddin's magic. He hoped that by continuing to shadow the monk he would also have the opportunity to prove James did not have that power. If he did not, then disposing of his prey would become less complicated. Freoric would be more than ready for that assignment.

Thomas recognized the elf by the feel of his magic. He'd known Freoric was lurking around for days, but he hadn't mentioned it to James. Thomas walked out of the water and onto the bank of the pond, sitting down to dry his feet and put his sandals back on. The elf was still hiding somewhere behind him when he called out, "Freoric, join me."

Freoric's voice carried from a distance, "How is it that you always know I am here, monk?"

"It's my gift. I sense magic when I'm in its presence. I recognized you by how your magic feels. It's an elven talent; surely it doesn't surprise you? Please, join me. We don't need to be enemies. I've got a sandwich and an orange here for lunch, if you'd care to share."

Freoric walked to stand off to Thomas's side. "I'll not break bread with you, abomination."

"As you say, but I'll keep up extending the invitation. I hope someday we'll be friends."

"I am not your friend. I am your assassin, and I am only waiting for the permission that I know will someday come to follow through on what I am."

"I continue to believe that someday you'll welcome me to your home as an equal. Someday, I'll earn your respect as Myrddin earned the respect of your ancestors; you will be glad to welcome me as a loyal ally."

Freoric snorted in disgust, turned, and walked away.

CHAPTER FOURTEEN
We're Off To See The Wizard

THOMAS ARRIVED BACK AT the apartment to find a note from James letting him know that he was at Lizbet's and might be home a little late. Thomas didn't need the note from James to know that he was next door with the queen, but Thomas knew James wouldn't like it if Thomas showed up at Lizbet's simply because he sensed them there. The note, however, offered an invitation, a "come get me if you need something" indicator.

He was sure that James would want to know about the run-in with Freoric immediately; James had strongly cautioned him about interacting with the elves. He'd promised, and he didn't want to upset his friend again.

Thomas knocked lightly on the door at the neighbor's house. James answered before Thomas had to knock again.

"Thomas, what do you need?"

"An elf was following me today."

"What? The elves followed us here? Yeah, come in. I have to check on Lizbet, but I want to hear about this. Just keep it down because she needs her sleep."

Thomas seated himself on the couch in the Moore's living room while James went upstairs. When he returned he sat down on the other end of the coach and angled himself toward Thomas, "So, go. Tell me what happened."

"I went to the park this morning to gather starweed, and I sensed that the wisps were not the only magical presence around the pond. Then, I recognized the magic—it was Freoric, the elf who stalked us in London. So I called to him, and he showed himself."

James shook his head, "The elders gave me their troth that they wouldn't follow us. It seems the word of the elves doesn't mean as much as it used to. I'm beginning to understand how much the fae were changed by their sentence to the shadow realm, Thomas. The elves have never lived in gentle ways, but in the old times they honored their pledges. What did he say to you?"

"Called me an abomination, said I'm not his friend, that he's my assassin and only waiting for permission to take my life."

"Did he give you any idea why he's holding back?"

"No, mate, that he did not do. I extended my hand in friendship, and he walked away."

"Yeah...you really need to stop doing that. Someday you'll extend that hand and he'll chop it off. You need to get a clue, Tom. Elves...not...your...friends."

A spark of anger flared in Thomas's eyes, "Are you treating me like I'm empty-headed again?"

"No, sorry...I didn't mean to talk to you that way. I'm just so frustrated that we did what the elders asked and they didn't keep their side of the deal...is Freoric still around somewhere close?"

Thomas closed his eyes and reached out with his magic for other magical presences. He found Freoric just within the space where his senses could reach, across the street from the Moore home.

"Yes. Across the way."

James stood up and said, "Call me if Lizbet comes downstairs or you hear any noise at all coming from upstairs. I'm going to have a talk with Freoric."

James opened the door and looked up and down the street for a trace of the elf. He spotted the tip of a bow over the top of a wide brick post at the entrance to a driveway across the street and walked toward it.

"You can come out, Freoric. Thomas will always know you're there."

The elf stood up and faced James.

James faced off with the elf, eyes narrowed. "The word of the elves meant something in Myrddin's time. I'm saddened to find it means nothing now."

"I was sent only to make sure that you kept the word you gave."

"And your people did this by breaking theirs? Times have changed when the elders dishonor themselves in this way." James stepped closer to the elf, trying to appear at least a little threatening, "Why would they take the risk of losing Myrddin's friendship through this action?"

"You yourself have said that you are not Myrddin. Perhaps you do not have either Myrddin's power or his wisdom."

"As you say. And then, perhaps I do. It's not something I need to prove to someone like you."

"Yet if you did, you would have no further trouble from me. I would return to my elders with proof that you have the power to keep the abomination in check."

James was tired of the patient words Myrddin's memories helped him speak. He didn't like having an armed elf prowling around outside of Lizbet's house, and he felt his neck reddening in anger, "Look, elf, I've told you that Thomas is under my protection. That's all you need to know."

Freoric's only response was to tuck an escaped lock of long black hair streaked with strands of gray behind his ear and laugh.

James felt himself boiling over and abruptly thrust his right hand straight out toward Freoric. The magic came to him as naturally as breathing. A bright ball of blue flame appeared in the outstretched hand.

"In my time, the appropriate expression for a situation like this is 'do you want a piece of me?'," James raised his other hand and a bolt of lightning lit the evening sky, "... so, tell me, elf, do you want a piece of me?"

As the bolt of lightning reached down from the clouds to paint a stripe from the heavens to James's fingertips, Freoric sunk slowly to one knee and bowed his head. "I apologize, Myrddin, for doubting you. I will communicate with the elders and advise them you have kept your word. I will no longer follow you or Thomas, but I may be required to remain here because of the presence of the queen."

Freoric then stood and walked down the street, his long braid swinging like a pendulum, counting the steps it took for him to reach the end of the street, turn, and then disappear from view.

James watched him go, not allowing the magic to

extinguish itself until the elf was out of sight. He dropped his hand to his side and then collapsed to sit on the grassy tree lawn.

"Och, that was quite a display, laddie. I love the scent of ozone, don't you?"

James turned to find Eamon behind him.

"I wasn't going to use Myrddin's magic. Ever. And then I thought about Lizbet and Bobby being right next door while an elven assassin stalked my room-mate, and I just lost it."

"I believe the elves will no longer doubt your power or your willingness to display it, though the lightning may have been a little over-the-top. My hair's still standing on end from the charge. Perhaps the ball of flame would have been enough?"

James looked at the gruagach and rolled his eyes. Eamon's hair stood out in all directions even without any electricity in the atmosphere.

"Why was the elf here, lad? I'm surprised there are any outside of Europe."

"He's probably the first, and hopefully, the only elf to visit Ohio." James said, "He says that he followed us to make sure that Thomas really left England and isn't returning, but I think there is something more to it than that. I don't think that Thomas is really out of danger from the elves, and I'm not sure that my blowing my top like that will be enough to keep them away, either."

"Laddie, the fae are falling apart without their queen. The races have been at peace for a long time, but the elves are now starting to make noise about increasing their power. Hamish told me that there are a number of the European fae who no longer feel secure that the elves will stay within their own boundaries. If ye recall, the elves have never needed a reason to make war."

"I don't see the point— how many of them are there? Forty, fifty thousand? It's ridiculous that they believe they can hold power in the modern world."

"Aye, but they're ambitious. They're stuck in olden times when magic beat anything that humans could do. They underestimate the power of human technology. They're wary of it, but they don't truly understand it. Unlike the rest of the fae, they haven't eavesdropped on humans on a regular basis. They despise humans to the extent that they haven't bothered to understand the enemy. That's always been their failing."

Thomas felt the power of the magic building as James spoke with the elf. He watched from just behind the picture window in the Moore's living room as the fireball lit the street and the lightning streaked down from the sky to touch James's fingertips and hang there. He held his breath, hoping that James would have no cause to let loose his power and do damage to his own relationship with the elves.

As Freoric turned and started to walk away, Thomas's breath rushed out of him in a great sigh of relief and awe. The lightning still blazed in the sky, illuminating the elf's retreat.

"He's magnificent, isn't he?" came a soft voice from behind him.

He didn't turn. He didn't want her to know she had caught him by surprise. "Yes. Magnificent. I'm proud to call him my grandfather."

"He is no more your grandfather than I am your grand-mother," the girl replied.

"That's true. And yet, I believe he feels that bond to me and views me as kin."

"Perhaps." The girl walked forward to stand beside him, dressed in a dark blue gown. "You'll leave before he returns, but I have one request of you before you go." She held out a piece of paper with druidic writing on its surface. "Make sure that you share the knowledge of this potion with Tanji. I want her to make it for Lizbet. Langoureth will be able to read it. Do not tell her where you got this knowledge."

Thomas was glad to obey any demand she made of him. "As you say, Morgan," he stretched out his hand to take the offered piece of paper and bowed his head slightly toward her, "I am your servant and will do as you request."

Thomas started to turn to leave by the front door, but she nodded toward the back and said, "That way. And should we speak again, see that you name me only as Lizbet."

Thomas nodded and walked through the family room, exiting onto the lightning-lit patio. As he hopped over the short fence between the yards, the night went black again.

Morgan arranged herself seductively on the couch, her feet up and a hip thrust out, her unbound hair spread across the couch pillows where she lay her head. She took a folded blanket off a cassock and covered herself with it loosely.

When she heard James walk into the living room, she feigned a sleepy look and asked, "Is everything okay? The lightning woke me up. I didn't like that Thomas was here, so I sent him away."

James perched on the edge of the coach where she lay

and shook his head. "Yes, I think it's okay now. And I get it about Thomas,"

"Good." She sat up and patted the couch next to where she sat. "You could come closer, if you want. I think a hero deserves a kiss. I saw how you stood up to that elf. I was proud of you."

James moved closer but expressed reluctance for the praise, "*I'm* not proud of me. I went too far. I didn't need to use that much magic simply to prove a point. And, truthfully, I was sure that if he'd said the wrong thing, he wouldn't have had much to say to anyone anymore because he'd be a grease spot on the pavement. I don't trust myself with this much magic."

The fae nuzzled his shoulder. "You'll use it exactly as you should use it. To protect me. You always have. I wouldn't have blamed you if you'd had to harm the elf to keep me safe." She leaned her face in close to his and kissed him gently.

James couldn't help but return her kiss.

Soon, her mouth moved against his more insistently, and her hands began to roam across his chest. She moved to lay back and pull him down on top of her, but he pushed her away.

When she looked up at him, his face wore an expression of anger and disgust.

"You're not Lizbet…how could I make that mistake? Lizbet might understand why I did what I had to do, but she would never praise me for nearly incinerating anyone, fae or not. And she definitely wouldn't want to make out in her living room when Bobby could be home from school any minute."

She reached out for him again, and he pushed her roughly away, "Stay away from me!"

* ~ * ~ *

Lizbet rushed to the surface of consciousness. She fell back on the couch, disoriented. James's eyes were angry, his mouth curled up in disgust. She couldn't understand what was happening. Why had he pushed her?

Frightened, she backed away from him, pulling the blanket with her. "James? Why are you so angry? How did I get here?"

James looked searchingly into her eyes, and then slowly sat down in the chair across from where she lay on the couch.

"I'm not angry with *you*...Morgan was here. I thought she was you...I, well, I wanted her to be you. And then I knew better. And she was very...she was very friendly."

"James, I'm so sorry! I knew if I fell asleep, she'd turn up. I just knew."

"Lizbet, I..." James stopped, pausing too long without continuing.

"What? Whatever it is, you can tell me."

"Lizzie, I can't be alone with you until this is over. I can't risk thinking I'm with you when I'm with her instead. Do you understand?"

Unfortunately, Lizbet did understand. It made her sick to think of Morgan's hands on her boyfriend while she was stuck in her own head, unconscious. Her heart tightened painfully when she pictured it. "Yeah...I definitely do."

"As soon as your mom gets home, I'm taking off. And I'm not going to be around you unless there is someone else there, too. I don't know what else to do."

Lizbet lay her head down on a couch pillow and closed her eyes tight. She wasn't going to cry; she wouldn't give Morgan that satisfaction, but man...that fae had to go.

~~*

James stopped in quickly at the apartment and told Thomas not to expect him for dinner. He didn't want to talk about anything that had just happened with his elf-loving, fae-worshipping room-mate and just said, "Later..." when Thomas asked how he was. He didn't care that Thomas looked hurt.

He quickly shoved some of his Renaissance Faire gear into a large duffel bag, including his heavy combat sword, along with his armor and helmet. As he walked downstairs, he dialed through the list of his SCA group contacts until he found one who could meet him later at the practice grounds.

He might be Myrddin to the fae, but tonight he'd be an anonymous knight, working off his anger in swordplay.

~~*

Thomas left a message for Tanji to pick up after school. He hoped that the temptation of learning new magic would be enough to encourage her to stop by on her way home. He hoped she would arrive with a little bit of pixie dust and a large amount of curiosity.

He was confidently setting things up in the kitchen when Tanji called back.

"Hey, Thomas! It would be great to be able to make something to help Lizbet out, especially if she suggested it herself. I'll grab the pixie dust and swing by after dinner."

When Tanji arrived, Thomas was making a show of

puzzling over the ancient druidic writing in the spell he'd gotten from the internet. He said, "I can't read the old language. I remember a little, which kind of surprised me, but I guess that would be some of what came over from Faolan's knowledge even though I don't have his memories. That's how I knew we'd need the pixie dust and some of the other stuff, but the rest of it has me stumped."

Tanji read slowly through the formula for the potion and then looked at what he already had out on the counter. "It looks like the only thing missing is elk horn. That's not good. Do you have any elk horn?"

"I do, actually. I picked it up in London in a 'magic' shop when I was staying there. Apparently, faux witches have always liked the stuff for aphrodisiacs. I don't have any experience of them, but I understand that the power that comes from feelings of love and passion can be energizing."

Tanji turned to look him directly in the eyes and said, "No experience at all, Thomas? What a shame—based on my limited experience at this point, I think you'd like them."

It seemed as if the small kitchen had shrunk instantly to a much smaller size. Thomas quickly turned away to pull the mortar and pestle out of an overhead cabinet, not sure why he felt flushed. He was suddenly as aware of Tanji's physical presence as he was of her magic.

CHAPTER FIFTEEN
Inside Out

BOBBY TURNED AROUND AND looked down at the five adult gnomes who were following him. Gurdenn was in the group, as were Kaluum, Dracorr, and two of the younger gnomes whose names he couldn't pronounce. They smiled up at him, and he smiled back.

"Okay, you guys", Bobby said, "you have to go back home now. You can't come to school with me again. I'll get in trouble if you do."

The gnomes just kept smiling and made no effort to leave. Then, the smallest gnome broke out in an energetic dance around his feet, and soon the others joined in. When the school bus pulled up, Bobby stomped a foot down hard to get their attention.

"Go HOME!" he shouted. The gnomes scurried back the way they'd come, but as soon as Bobby disappeared into the bus, they ran back in a clump, jostling against each other as they went, and jumped onto the back bumper as it pulled away. Kaluum lost his grip and fell into the road, scrambling out of the way of an oncoming car just in time. The other four held on tight as the bus pulled out of sight.

* ~ * ~ *

"No, girl, you do not want to wear your shirt to school that way, I promise you," Tanji said as Lizbet slid into the passenger seat of the car.

Lizbet looked down at her v-neck t-shirt, "Why? What's wrong with it?"

"Nothing—if you're into the inside-out look."

Lizbet's eyes darted to the shoulder seams on her shirt. "Man...I'm so tired now that I can't even dress myself. There's no way I can fix this quickly with wings, so I'll be back." Lizbet got out of the car and walked back up to the house, returning in a few minutes with her shirt on right side out.

"You didn't sleep again last night?"

"No, I slept. But I kept waking up to check that I was still me and still in my own bed...so, not a great sleep. Maybe four hours, tops. But I did get a pretty good nap yesterday when James picked me up from school."

"You going to pass out every day just to see more of him?" Tanji asked, a note of teasing in her voice.

"Nope. Wouldn't work anyway—James says he can't be alone with me anymore."

"Huh? Why?"

"Because yesterday Morgan came on to him, and he mistook her for me," Lizbet grimaced, "...yeah, that's right, the fae who is trying to take over my body wants my boyfriend, too. Pretty soon the two of you will be BFFs and

QUEEN OF THE FAE 143

hang out laughing about poor old Lizbet who couldn't even dress herself."

"No, I don't think so. Langoureth sensed her immediately the last time she tried to trick me. They were best friends for like sixty years, and then, after the fae were sent to the shadow realm, they grew more and more distant over time. Morgan was very sad for a long time, but then her sadness turned to bitterness and anger. By the time you freed the fae, all she really cared about was the power. She was nothing like Morgan started out to be. Eamon says it's 'cause she's a nymph and was unable to bear being parted from her one true love."

"That's a very romantic story. But she's not getting him back. And I'm not sharing."

"But wow...you can't be alone with him?"

"Well, you'll hang out with us, won't you, so we can be in the same room? And I think James wants me to include Thomas more, anyway. I'm not thrilled about that one, but if that's the only way I can see him, then that's how it'll be. All the old ladies in here will just have to deal with it, no matter how much they hated Faolan."

"I guess that's one thing Morgan's other lives share with the fae Morgan. You were supposed to kill him, you know, not just destroy his amulet. It's what she promised everyone."

"Yeah, but I don't have that kind of hate. The human Morgan didn't want me to kill him—just destroy him, which I definitely did when I took his memories away. Faolan is gone. Maybe the human Morgan would have been more like her fae side turned out if her life had gone differently. I mean, the human Morgan only has that one thing that makes her crazy, that Faolan thing, but what if

Myrddin had died when she was young? Maybe she would have been a different person, too."

"Maybe." Tanji parked the car and stowed the keys in her oversized bag. Then she pulled out a bottle filled with an evil-looking, chunky, brownish-green liquid and handed it to Lizbet. "Surprise! Here's that solution to the sleepy-all-the-time problem you asked for. Guaranteed to keep you awake for at least two hours at a time. Just a couple of swigs should do it when you're feeling drowsy."

"Seriously? You're the best. Is it going to be another one of those things I'm going to wish I never got a taste of?"

"Absolutely. You won't see me putting it anywhere near my mouth. But it should do the trick. I guess you have to ask yourself how bad you want to stay awake."

"I'm trying not to sleep unless I have a really reliable watcher, so maybe this will help. Do you think I can crash at your's for a while after school while you study?"

"Yeah, we could do it at my house. The daddio will still be out working."

"Cool, so let's see how well this stuff is going to work." Lizbet uncorked the bottle and put it up to her lips, taking a quick swallow. "Oh yeah, vile. Really vile."

Bobby was glad to be back at school after having been away for a week. He missed his friends, especially his best buddy Kyle, whose face lit up when he spotted Bobby getting on the bus. Bobby hurried to sit down next to him, pulling a comic book out of his bag to share with his friend as they rode along. Kyle liked to do all of the voices, and the girl voices especially cracked Bobby up. Girls don't really sound like that, but it was funny anyway.

When the bus stopped, Kyle bobbed along slightly behind Bobby, his red backpack scraping the ground. Then Kyle stumbled suddenly, and he fell onto one knee, crying out as he hit the pavement.

"Kyle! Are you okay?" Bobby asked. As he turned around to his friend, he thought he caught a glimpse of a gnome running swiftly away to disappear around the corner of the building.

Kyle sat on the ground holding his leg, his lower lip jutting out and his eyes scrunched close, trying not to cry. One of the teachers approached him.

"Kyle, what happened here?"

"I tripped, Mrs. Johnson. But my knee really hurts."

"We'll get you into the nurse, and she'll fix it right up. Can you walk okay?" she asked as she helped him up.

"Yes, I think so," Kyle said, as he followed the teacher into the school, limping.

Bobby watched his friend go, and then walked to the corner of the building and looked around it—nothing there. He was probably just seeing things. Why would a gnome want to trip his friend?

From his perch in a tree in front of the school, Eamon had watched the gnome trip Bobby's young friend and then streak away. The rest had spread out around the school yard, and Eamon had no trouble finding them with his highly developed sense of smell, but he wouldn't have been able to locate them just by sight. They'd done a good job of hiding.

While Eamon knew that the gnomes wouldn't hurt Bobby, he wasn't certain that they weren't a threat to the other children in the school if Bobby was threatened. After school started for the day, Eamon jumped down from his tree and walked around to the back of the school to talk to the gnome chief, Gurrdenn. It was time to start to make sense of this.

～～*

Tanji answered the door and looked down to see Eamon standing there, his hat in hand. She knew from previous visits that this meant he expected to be invited in. He'd explained it was customary in "olden times" for men to remove their hats inside a building. It seemed like a silly rule to her. It was also alarming to answer the door and look down into a wiry mass of dark hair standing straight up from the gruagach's scalp. Like most people, Tanji wished that Eamon would keep his cap on.

"Hey, little dude, what's up?"

"We've a problem that I'd like to discuss about Bobby Moore."

"Cool, but keep it down. Lizbet is trying to get in a nap up in my room. She's paranoid about Morgan taking her over when she sleeps, so I have to go up and check on her in a while."

"Good. I don't really want to worry her anyway."

Tanji led him to the kitchen table, and Eamon hopped onto one of the chairs across from her, his head just barely visible above the table top. Tanji had to smile. If anyone had told her a year ago that she'd be regularly hanging out with a fifteen hundred year old fairy with a permanent bad hair day, she would have thought they were nuts. Now, it was just an ordinary thing. Amazing how quickly a person can adapt.

"Lassie, we need to put our heads together about

this—I've spoken to the gnome chief, and I now think that the gnomes may be dangerous to Bobby and his friends. From what I can gather, they don't like their god bein' free to roam around, leaving them godless at the burrow."

"Yeah, well...maybe they should go back to worshipping ceramic garden gnomes. Problem solved."

Eamon shook his head, "It's not that easy, lass. The gnomes took Bobby as their god when he intervened with Morgan and saved two of their huddle from her violence. Unless someone or something comes along to offer them something of more value, they won't shift their allegiance away from him."

"What can we do, then?"

"I wondered if there were a spell you know of to keep them close to the burrow. Today at the school, they injured one of Bobby's little friends with a prank. I think that they may go farther out of jealousy if they continue to follow him."

"Really? They're picking on little kids now?"

"To be fair, the kids are quite big to the gnomes, but they don't recognize how fragile a human child can be. Their only experience is of their own children, who are tough as a dragon's hide from birth."

"I don't know, Eamon, I'm not channeling anything right off the bat. I'll probably need some help...James maybe?"

"Aye, but if we tell James, Lizbet would know. And then poor Sheila as well. But...I suppose it's better to be honest about the threat."

"Yes, Eamon, I think so. I know Lizbet won't want to get her mom any more worried than she already is, but telling her is the right thing. I mean, I've certainly done my share of putting one over on the parents, but Bobby just isn't old enough to take care of himself."

From the hall, Lizbet said, "Ha! Seriously, *you're* saying 'let's tell the parents'? Wow. Times have changed."

"How long have you been there, lassie?"

"Long enough, Eamon. We've been through this like fifty times—if you think you need to do things to protect me, you should really be talking to me about them instead of just going out and doing them."

"I know, lassie, but I'm a fae. Tricksiness is in my nature. I can't change with the snap of my fingers. I'm tryin' to improve."

"Yeah, just...try harder. It's not like you come up with all your secret plans for some nefarious reason, so just be honest about them. And Tanj...you're keeping secrets from me, too?"

"If I pointed out that I'm half-fae now and therefore half-tricksy, would I get a pass?"

"Nope."

"Didn't think so. So...sorry, girl. But you know you're a hot mess these days, right?"

"Yep. And my best friends scheming behind my back when my little brother is in trouble doesn't really help me, does it?"

"No," Tanji walked to her friend and hugged her. "Are you feeling more rested?"

"I am, a little."

Tanji heard the van pulling into the garage and announced, "The paternal unit has now arrived home, and James should be with him, so there's no reason we can't grab him, pile into the Tanjmobile, get ourselves over to wizard central, and figure this bad boy out."

* ~ * ~ *

With five of them gathered in the small living room which doubled as Thomas's bedroom, things were cramped. Lizbet sat down close to James, but he got up and moved away, uncomfortable with the closeness after what had happened with Morgan the night before.

Tanji consulted her spell book, lips pursed, running her finger quickly down the page as she skimmed for anything that could help with the problem. Thomas sat beside her on the arm of the couch, looking over her shoulder.

James suspected Thomas of trying to memorize everything he saw in the book while trying not to be obvious— Thomas was that way, he wanted to know every possible thing there was to know about magic and thought about almost nothing else. James had hoped that getting to know more people who had interests other than magic would help with that, but so far, no luck. He knew Lizbet didn't want to encourage Tanji's interest in Thomas, but James was all for anything that could get him away from the potion factory once in a while.

Tanji looked up from the book, "Truthfully, it seems like the thing that would help us the most here would to actually be gnomes. A gnome could easily whip up a barrier that lets everything pass through from either direction except a gnome. But other than that...I got nothin'."

Thomas walked to the kitchen as the tea pot started to whistle. He took it off the burner and then turned back to the group, "What if we *could* use gnome magic?"

"Sure. You got a gnome in your pocket ready to do us a favor?" James asked. His mouth turned up at the corners a little when he heard the girls giggle. Thomas's expression remained as sober as ever.

"No. But I think we could trick a gnome into casting that spell with the right kind of encouragement. Because there *is* a spell in Tanji's book for 'gnome-enthralling', and another one that we could use to erase the memory of doing it once the spell was cast. If the gnome didn't remember doing the spell, there would be no one to undo it."

Eamon nodded his head in agreement. "Aye...that plan might work, lad. And you're not even a full half-fae, then? I'd say that plan's worthy of the tricksiest amongst us. What does the enthralling involve?"

Tanji skimmed back through the book and then read quickly through a page, "Not much—basically get the gnome to drink a simple potion. and you throw in a couple of Gaelic charm words. Unfortunately, I haven't got any ideas about how we'd get one of them to drink it."

"Och, I see no problem with that part of the plan. Who wants to help me capture a gnome?"

James said, "I do it for a living, but these gnomes don't respond to the lures."

"Nothin' that complicated, lad. Have you got a bag of sugar? Gnomes go crazy for it. We'll just lay out a line of it from one of the burrows, and when one of them follows it into the woods, I'll grab him, and you can pour that potion right down his gullet."

"Eamon, you're not going to hurt the gnome, are you?" asked Lizbet, rubbing her eyes and yawning. "I know you don't like gnomes, but I also don't want to see any of them get hurt during this. I just want them under control so that Bobby is safe."

"No fear, lassie. A gnome is no problem for me. Plus, they've got quite tough skins. We could tussle all day and the gnome would walk away without a scratch."

"Okay then, I'll help out with that part of it," said James, "Thomas, have you got the potions under control?"

"Yes. But there are additional things I need. A toad,

for one, for the amnesia spell. Actually, just one particular gland. I'll need to find a living one if we want this to work."

"Okay, ewwww," Lizbet said, "...wait, I know this spell from Morgan...doesn't it also need a pixie feather?"

Tanji replied, "Not a pixie feather specifically, just a faerie feather. So...do you mind?" Tanji moved toward her with one hand out.

"Really? You're plucking me?"

"Yeah, really. So, turn around, and I'll make it quick."

Lizbet turned around and Tanji tugged a small feather out from the end of one of Lizbet's wings. Lizbet winced just a little and then turned around again.

"Thanks," Tanji said.

"No prob. It's for Bobby, so take 'em all if you need 'em."

Tanji headed into the kitchenette with the feather. Thomas was already setting out supplies. Together, they inventoried what they had, and then Thomas announced he would be going out to the local pond while Tanji mixed up a slurry from some of the ingredients they already had.

CHAPTER SIXTEEN
I Talk To The Trees

SHEILA TRIED NOT TO stare at the complex headdress of leaves the visitor at the front door wore, but it was so exotic and stunning it was nearly impossible not to. Other than the green leaves and willow twigs entwined throughout the woman's very black, straight hair, she was ordinary; a pretty oriental woman whom Sheila judged to be in her early thirties, wearing no makeup, loose jeans, tennis shoes, and a baggy sweatshirt.

"Hi. My name is Mona. I hope I'm not disturbing you, but I wondered if I could talk to Lizbet Moore? It's taken me a long time to get here, and I really need to see her."

"I'm afraid my daughter's not here. Does she know you?"

"No. But, I think you can probably tell this, right? I'm half-fae, and I'm going crazy trying to understand all of this. My fae side keeps insisting that the queen can help me. And your daughter, she's Morgan, the Queen of the Fae. I need her help."

Sheila had turned away other half-fae who had come looking for Lizbet, but this woman looked so tired, so distressed. "My daughter is a junior in high school who can't even play on her own track team. She isn't queen of anything."

The young woman stood there, looking disappointed and very tired.

Sheila softened. "Look, I don't think she can help you, but she'll be home in an hour or so. You can come back then, if you want to talk to her."

"Thank you! I've come all the way from New Mexico, and I...it's just been very hard. It's not like I can hide what I am."

Sheila felt her heart go out to the younger woman. "Look, why don't you come in and wait? Coffee?"

"Coffee? Are you sure? Because that would be amazing."

Sheila moved back, holding the door wide so that Mona could enter. "My name is Sheila, by the way."

* ～ * ～ *

Lizbet walked home from next door in a haze, her tired eyes ready to close and her brain completely fogged in. She was too exhausted to even notice that her mother had company as she plodded past the kitchen on her way to the stairs.

"Lizbet?" her mother called, "Could you come into the kitchen? You have a visitor."

She turned back to the kitchen nook and lifted her feet with effort as she shuffled back the way she came.

"Sweetie, this is Mona Collins, she's come from New Mexico to meet you."

"Hey," said Lizbet.

Mona went to one knee and bowed her head.

Lizbet just looked down at her, too tired to make a remark or to ask why she did what she did. Her mother stepped in, "Mona came to consult with you as Queen of the Fae. I told her that you probably can't help her."

"Oh...that," Lizbet said, "Mona, please get up. Morgan was definitely queen, but I don't have her memories. I'm sorry."

"But, please...don't turn me away. I've come to serve within your court as my fae half did in the shadow realm. No one wants me anymore. No one wants a half fae. I can't disguise what I am like some of the others can do. It's not like I can prune myself like a tree. I've tried. It's terribly, terribly painful to even remove one twig. I'll never trim another hedge as long as I live."

"Look, I'm really sorry about what's happened, but..."

"Please, please help me understand this...you must know something about it. What it's like not to be normal anymore? To not have the choice? I hear voices in my head whenever I'm outside walking on the grass, or when I touch a tree. I don't understand it. It's so horrible."

Lizbet nodded her head and tried to push out the fogginess. "Give me just a minute, okay? I need to use the bathroom."

She took her backpack into the bathroom with her and took out the bottle of viscous, chunky liquid Tanji had given her. She closed her eyes tight and then threw back her head, put it to her lips, and took a big swig of the foul-smelling stuff. Within seconds, she began to wake up as the powerful, warm brightness of it coursed through her veins.

When she returned from the bathroom, she was much, much perkier.

"Okay, so...you said that you came here because you needed your queen—why?"

"I served you in the Fae realm—well, my fae did. Her name was Euphemia—do you remember her?"

Lizbet shook her head. "No—no memories of that. My fae half...let's just say that the Queen doesn't play nice with others. I don't know why you'd be hearing voices. As much as I want to, I really can't help you."

Lizbet's mother freshened Mona's coffee and asked her, "What arrangements have you made for tonight?"

"I haven't made any yet. I have a little money, but it won't last me more than a month or two. I planned to stay, if only to be in a town where there's someone else like me. Where I lived for all my life, they pretty much told me I'm not wanted there anymore."

Mom nodded her head, wearing her sympathetic face. "Yes, I understand that. Lizbet and I have had a few run-ins ourselves with people who can't really understand. Her father included."

Lizbet tapped her fingers on the table, jittery. She was beginning to feel extremely revved up, and her thoughts moved quickly. She wanted to help, and then she realized that she could, if only in a non-magical way.

"Mona, if you could get a job working with other people who either have magic or are accepting of magic, would that be something you'd want to do?"

"Yes, if I could. I'd give anything to be around others who understand. I was a reporter for my small-town paper until no one was willing to talk to me anymore, but I'm not proud—I'll do just about anything at this point to keep body and soul together."

"Okay, hang on, let me make a call." Lizbet hit speed dial for Tanji's number.

"Tanj...is your dad still looking for workers?"

Tanji replied, "Yeah, I think so. With the shop opening up soon and more business every day from farther away, he was talking about trying to find more people."

"Okay, 'cause I've got someone who would be really happy to have the job."

"Let me ask..." Lizbet could hear Tanji talking to her father and then Tanji returned to the phone, "Yeah, he says have him at the house Monday morning at 8 AM, because he's got plenty of work. He'll give him a trial."

"Actually, it'll be a she, her name is Mona..." Lizbet directed her next question to Mona, "Can you be ready to work at 8 AM next Monday?"

"Uh, sure. I can do that."

"Cool!" Lizbet put the phone back up to her mouth, "Mona will meet your dad then. I'll fill her in on the deets."

As Lizbet wrote down Tanji's address for Mona, she felt good about what she'd accomplished without even being a queen.

Mona stayed for dinner and arranged a hotel room for the rest of the week while she looked for somewhere more permanent if the job with the Gnome Removal service worked out. She'd stayed to watch TV when invited, but she and Sheila had spent more time talking than watching. Sheila thought she was an interesting, intelligent woman.

Sheila noticed her daughter beginning to yawn again around nine o'clock, and within minutes, Lizbet was fast asleep on the couch. Sheila walked Mona to the door, and said, "Please feel free to stop by again. I enjoyed talking tonight. I don't know many adults who understand about all of this."

Mona smiled then, her first unstressed smile of the evening. "I enjoyed meeting you, too. Maybe we could get together for coffee or something once I'm settled in. That's assuming you know someplace where people won't gawk at me."

"I think people will probably gawk anywhere, but I'd be happy to be there for moral support if they do. Lizbet still gets that whenever she goes someplace new, but she seems to be learning to deal with it, I think. Well, I hope, really. Maybe you can, too."

"I'm trying. But it's not that easy. I put so much hope in the queen knowing what all my weird experiences are about."

"I'm really sorry that Lizbet can't help with that, but I do wish you wouldn't call her 'Queen'—she's just my daughter, that's all. A little different to look at than before, but she's still just my Lizbet," Sheila said. As Mona turned to walk to her car she added, "Lizbet gave you our number, right? Don't hesitate to call. And let's make sure we meet for that coffee soon."

Sheila realized as Mona left how glad she was to have spent time talking with another adult without having to duck around the issues of fae-ness. It had been a while since the elephant in the room wasn't always present when she was talking to people at work or in the neighborhood. Most of them were polite, but she could sense they were often holding back, maybe trying to get away as quickly as possible. She tried to remain upbeat, but it was difficult. She hoped she'd made a new friend who could understand.

Sheila went back to the living room and covered her sleeping daughter with a light blanket before going off to sleep herself. She didn't have the heart to wake her up and make her go to bed.

Mona was startled when Lizbet dropped into existence in the hotel room as she walked through the door with her suitcases in tow. She stood there, stunned, until Lizbet spoke.

"The girl didn't require that you bend your knee, but I require more from those who serve me, Euphemia."

"Morgan, I didn't know you, I'm sorry..." Mona dropped to one knee, her head bowed deeply, "...please forgive me."

"You are forgiven this time. It's been a long time since anyone but my gruagach has bent the knee to me. I like that there are still those who recognize the need of it. I may look different than I did, but I'm still your queen, and you, Euphemia, have a skill that I need to allow me to communicate quickly across the continents."

"I'm not sure what you mean, mistress."

"Come with me, and you'll understand soon enough."

Mona lifted up and followed Morgan as she led out into the park beyond the hotel. When they were well hidden in the darkness among the trees, Morgan told her to stand still, take off her shoes, and reach with her roots for the soil.

Mona meekly replied, "I don't know what you mean."

"Yes, you do. Allow Euphemia to take charge. Follow deeply into her memories. You've been reaching for the soil all along. You just didn't know that the whispering of all the connected voices was coming from your magic as a dryad. You're a nymph with the power of the trees to communicate across long distances by your connection to the earth. It's probably been confusing for you, but you can learn to reach out for individual voices if you let your fae half take the lead."

"I can try."

As she pushed her toes into the cold soil, she began to remember. Mona gasped as the voices of the other dryads reached out to her. She felt her body transforming, connecting to the earth, and along with it, the horrible, racking pain.

From outside of her agony, she heard Morgan say, "I believe in you, Euphemia. When you've mastered your ability, you'll be more than useful to me."

CHAPTER SEVENTEEN
Don't Fence Me In

JUST BEFORE DAWN, EAMON spread a trail of sugar from one of the burrow holes off into the woods. With a little luck, it would lure only one of the gnomes his way. If more than one found the trail, it would be difficult to manage. He didn't know if they'd have enough amnesia potion for more than three.

He and James lay silently on the ground among the tall green ferns, waiting for one of the gnomes to exit the burrow in the first light of false dawn and catch the scent. It wasn't long before one of the elder gnomes popped his head out of the burrow, nose twitching. Greedy thing that he was, he exited the burrow, turned around, placed his small rear end over the burrow entrance, and blew out a great load of gas to keep his huddle-mates from sniffing the treat before he'd scooped it all up for himself.

Eamon was poised at the ready as the gnome approached

them and sprung from his hiding place to grab the gnome, placing a hand over his mouth from behind while James uncorked the potion.

"Alright, then, if you know what's good for ye, you'll not try to rouse your huddle when I remove my hand from your mouth. You know who that lad is, right?" Eamon said, as he nodded toward James, "The great sorcerer Myrddin, that's who he is. He doesn't *want* to hurt you, but you know that he could."

The gnome nodded solemnly, his eyes wide with fear.

"Good. Myrddin has something for ye. Drink it down without a fuss, right?"

The gnome nodded again.

Eamon removed his hand from the gnome's mouth, and James handed the potion down to it. "All of it, now. It won't harm you."

His eyes still wide, the gnome never removed his gaze from James's face as he drank the potion. The effect was immediate. Eamon let him go as he suddenly relaxed and started giggling quietly, sitting down on the grass.

Eamon told the gnome what he expected him to do, and the gnome walked a circuit around the Moore's backyard with James and Eamon following behind. He chanted, farted, and burped as he went. Eamon had never been sure if the bodily functions were an important part of magic for the gnomes or if they just couldn't control it, even for their rituals. Not that gnomes are big on mystical. They're earthy creatures with very simple needs: food, shelter, safety, and gods to cover the bases for everything else. It doesn't get more basic than that.

When the gnome was done, Eamon had him sit back down in the grass and handed him the memory potion, advising him to drink. When the gnome finished off every drop, Eamon took the bottle from him, and he and James quickly walked past the porch, around the side of the garage, then out to the driveway where they parted with an enthusiastic fist bump.

Eamon knew that the gnome, when he woke up with his small leather pouch now full of sugar, wouldn't pause to wonder how he'd gotten so lucky to come across such a rare treat. Gnomes aren't smart enough to ask the really big questions. Or even the really small ones.

Through the sliding glass door at the back patio of the Moore house, Gurrdenn watched Bobby eat his breakfast, kiss his mother, and then grab his backpack and walk toward the front door. He called out to the others, and they joined him as he headed for the gate at the side of the yard.

The gnomes were moving fast when they slammed against the invisible barrier. There were many cries of pain and a great deal of gnomish cursing. A few minutes later, they'd recovered their normally upbeat approach to problems and took another run at the barrier.

After the fourth attempt, getting the same result every time, Gurrdenn walked back to the burrow, trailed by his huddle-mates. He sat on the flat stone that served as the place of law-giving. The others brought him food and drink while he sat and pondered in front of the azaleas.

When Lizbet's alarm went off, she woke up feeling groggy and light-headed with just a touch of a headache. She felt the pull of a small craving. It wasn't hunger. In fact, she didn't feel hungry at all. When her eyes lit on the small brown bottle on the table, it occurred to her that it was just the thing. There was still at least three-fourths of a bottle of the stuff, so she would have plenty to make it through school this week. But she definitely needed to talk to Tanji about getting more.

Once the potion hit her system, she felt brilliantly alive. She bounded from bed with a song and dance. When she joined Bobby for breakfast, she gave him an extra portion of noogies. Oh, what a beautiful day!

She was bopping down the hallway at school when the shakes hit. She felt awful. Suddenly, she was so sleepy she felt sick. She sunk to the floor next to a set of lockers and rummaged through her backpack, looking for the brown bottle she'd made sure to store there before she left the house.

There were gray spots swirling before her eyes, and she sank lower onto the floor, but then...she found the bottle... it was such an effort to raise it to her lips...and then...oh, brilliant day. The warmth of it flowed through her and she felt like she could fly.

Feeling that she could, she did.

She laughed at the other students as they ran to get out of her way when she buzzed down the center of the hall, flapping her wings vigorously just for show.

"Ha! Why walk when you can fly? I'm having the BEST day!"

Miss Armstrong stood in the middle of the hall near the gym, talking to one of the girls on the track team. As the other students got out of the way noisily, she looked up and then turned to plant herself firmly in Lizbet's way.

"Moore! What's gotten into you? Feet on the floor! Now!"

Lizbet stopped then, and hung in the air for a moment, unsure about what was happening. She still felt pumped, better than she'd ever felt. And maybe that was the problem. She lowered her feet to the floor.

Miss Armstrong called down the hall. "Anyone hurt?"

There were headshakes, and a few students quietly answered "no".

"Moore, you're lucky this time. But, I think from now on we can agree that in addition to no running in the halls, there'll be no flying. Understood?"

Lizbet nodded her head. "Yes, Miss Armstrong. I was just feeling so good, I didn't think about it until I was doing it."

"No excuses, young lady. You should have known better."

"Yes," Lizbet said, "I'm sorry."

She was distracted through the rest of the school day, not able to pay attention to much, but she still felt like there was nothing she couldn't do. Maybe she was too confident. Or maybe everybody was just jealous, which is why they gave her a wide berth and strange looks. Which was stupid, because she had so much to say to everyone that it rushed out of her when anyone would listen.

She laughed and joked and slapped people she barely knew on the back in greeting in-between classes. A little too hard, maybe. But hey, if it was, they could just suck it up. Nothing could wreck this beautiful, glorious day.

The shakes hit her again, violently, when she was in the girl's bathroom after her last class. She quickly pulled the precious bottle out of her backpack, but her hands were so unsteady she lost hold of it. She cried out in frustration and tried to catch it, but she bobbled it, and it slipped through her hands.

It bounced against the edge of the counter as it fell and shattered as it hit the hard tile floor. Lizbet stared at it, still shaking, until she followed it down and dropped unconscious into the spreading pool of potion and shattered glass.

Morgan held a hand over the girl's arm where there was a deep gash, bleeding freely. The wound closed as a pale blue light glowed from the fae's open palm. Better. It would not do to have the Queen of the Fae greeting her followers bloodied.

She stood up, looking down at the mess the girl had made of things. She could feel many small cuts and a painful bump on her head. *She's freed me, at least,* she thought. *I am more than glad that Thomas suggested that potion to Langoureth. Too bad he didn't know it would have side effects. Perhaps I should have mentioned them when I gave it to him?* Morgan smiled to herself.

As a group of girls entered the bathroom, she turned to face them. One of them asked, "Lizbet, you okay?"

"I think you'll find I'm better than ever," Morgan replied, as she faded into the aether.

She popped back to Lizbet's house to change her clothes, and after she'd cleaned herself up and approved her appearance in the mirror, she walked downstairs and waved her hand across several pieces of furniture, reshaping them into styles more suitable to a queen. The house would do for her court for now. She didn't want to return to Scotland without Myrddin, and she would have to be happy with having him next door until he was ready to leave for home with her. She felt sure that she could convince the girl's mother that this is what an integrated version of Lizbet would be like. It would be difficult, though, to pretend to have the innocence of the girl, even for a short time. Still, it had to be. Declaring herself as Morgan would lose her

Myrddin and turn many humans against her. Neither of these things suited her plans.

She'd dressed in some of Lizbet's clothes instead of her own. She would eventually start dressing to her own tastes, but until everyone accepted her as Lizbet, she would have to be careful. The changes to the furniture would be enough for now. She had to make those changes: she would soon be holding court for her subjects.

The front doorbell rang. She opened the door, hands free, as a queen would. Faolan, no...Thomas, stood before her. He dropped to one knee, but he did not bow his head. Instead he looked up at her, his gaze one of adoration.

"I felt you here, my queen. I knew it was you."

The Fae didn't quite know what to do with him. He'd been a danger to Myrddin in the past, but she knew he was no threat now, and certainly, he was easily misled. Otherwise, he wouldn't be here looking up at her as he offered himself to serve.

"You may rise. Yes, I've integrated now. Please, call me Lizbet, for that is who I am. But I am Lizbet *and* Queen of the Fae."

Thomas nodded and rose. She noticed he was at least a foot taller than she was and as handsome as Faolan had been. Faolan's beauty had been wasted when he joined the monastery. She remembered her petty desire for great-grand-children from him when she had a human side and her upset when he chose to serve the church as a celibate instead. How foolish it seemed now, when she had lived for so many hundreds of years. She needed no children and grandchil-dren to carry on her legacy, only this young body that had so recently been yielded to her.

"Thomas, if you are offering to serve, there may soon be a time when I have a request of you."

"Anything," he replied.

~~*

Sheila arrived home to a house full of fae. Mona was there, and an elf was also seated stiffly on the living room couch, his bow resting across his lap, looking ready for action if needed.

Lizbet sat in a large wooden and velvet chair where a recliner had sat that morning.

"Lizzie, what's going on?"

"Mom, welcome home. I would like to introduce my friends. You know Mona, or, as she was known in Morgan's court, Euphemia. This is Freoric; he's the representative of the elves in this country. They've come to pay their respects to me as their queen."

"If that's true, then you're not Lizbet." In the back of her mind, Sheila remembered her daughter's warning that the fae might be dangerous. She wished she'd thought before she'd blurted that out.

"I am. Don't worry. She...Morgan, I mean...has finally fully remerged. Today at school. She gave up trying to take over. It was really cool."

Sheila continued to look at her daughter for a long moment. "If you're Lizbet, then tell me, what does Lizbet most want out of life?"

"That's an easy one, if you're talking about what I most want right now—I want to be free of the wings so that everything can just get back to normal. Which, as you can see, is already done." Lizbet stood up and turned around. Sheila could see that she was right—the wings were gone. Not just folded on her daughter's back, but gone. Lizbet said, "Isn't it great? But I do have responsibilities to the fae. I can help people like Mona now."

Sheila enclosed her daughter in her arms when she came forward for a hug. She wanted to be happy for her, but she wasn't sure she should be. The girl in her arms felt and sounded like her daughter, but a part of her held back. Lizbet didn't just want her wings gone. They were only a symbol; what her daughter really wanted was a normal life back. Holding court was not part of any normal life that Sheila would have expected.

"Mom, Mona and I are going to take a walk in the woods. It's such a nice day. We have so many things to talk about, don't we, Mona?"

Mona turned and nodded to Sheila in affirmation, but Sheila saw her hesitate for the briefest second before she did. She wasn't sure what that hesitation meant, but she didn't like it.

"Sure, honey. Just be back in time for dinner."

Sheila waited until they disappeared into the trees at the back of the garden to pull her phone out.

The first time Morgan had made her reach for the earth, it had been invigorating as the power began to feed up through the soles of her feet, but then it grew painful as the connection to the soil grew stronger and she began to transform. Afterward, Morgan assured her that the pain would decrease in time as her human cells absorbed more of the transformative magic a dryad uses to join with the earth. But Mona didn't want to do it again. And she certainly didn't want to do it every time Morgan commanded it.

But that didn't matter: Mona had no a choice. She'd

sought out the queen as a better alternative to the gawking and judging of other people, and now she was an indentured servant assigned to build a relationship with Sheila so she could spy on Lizbet's friends and family. She was also expected to be available for the queen whenever she wanted to dial up the fae at her home in Scotland. The queen smiled sweetly and asked her for her help, but behind the smile was a command and a threat. Why couldn't Morgan just get a cell phone like everyone else?

"Here will be fine, Mona. We're far enough away from the house. No one will see."

Mona slipped off her sandals and dug her feet into the soft topsoil. She closed her eyes as the energy started moving from her feet to her legs and up her body, changing her as the whispers of the other dryads became stronger. The voice of the queen came to her more as a vibration than a sound: in dryad form, she no longer had ears. The queen fed her questions, and she relayed them to the others who lived in various parts of Europe. When the queen had asked all of her questions, she told Mona she could return. Mona visualized pulling her roots from the soil, painfully, excruciatingly, and the stiffness in her body gradually eased until she fully inhabited her human form again.

"So, Euphemia, the answers to my questions?"

Mona looked up from the ground where she lay in agony and began to relay what she had learned.

CHAPTER EIGHTEEN

Fakin' It

GURRDENN PEERED IN THE family room window, watching Bobby stare at colorful images as they flashed across the front of the picture box. Gurrdenn also enjoyed the images, and he laughed as one of the creatures on the screen hit another over the head with a hammer bigger than he was. But there was no point to it; neither of the creatures ate the other one when the battle was over. Even so, Gurrdenn enjoyed the battle as he kept an eye on his god.

He heard the sound of a bell and then the raised voices of the mother and father. He moved to the large glass door on the patio to better see what was happening. Everything that happened in the home of the god was of interest to the gnomes.

The father looked angry, shouting at the mother from just outside the door. Gurrdenn didn't understand all that he heard but, "around those fae again" and "you have an elf standing guard at the end of your driveway" and "I'm getting Bobby out of here" made sense to him.

Bobby walked into the hallway then. The father saw him and said, "Bobby, come here. You're staying at my house for a while."

The mother turned around. Her voice was quiet. "Bobby, please go to your room. You're not in trouble. I just need to speak with your father privately."

The father moved forward but the mother blocked his path as he said, "Bobby, come here."

Bobby turned around and went back the way he'd come in. Gurrdenn tracked him with his eyes until the boy disappeared out of the other side of the family room.

The mother and father became quieter, and then the mother shut the door and the father was gone.

Gurrdenn knew what he had to do. The Bobby god was under threat.

～～*

Tanji parked at the side of the road and walked into the meadow. The sun was just rising, and the grass glistened with a touch of dew. It was a beautiful and peaceful scene. She wished she could enjoy it.

"Eamon?" she called.

The gruagach appeared at her side in a blur of movement. "Mornin', lassie. What brings you here so bright and early?"

"Real problems, I think. Lizbet's mom called me last night, and she was worried. She says that Lizbet had an elf over for a pow-wow, and she was planning on 'holding court' regularly as Queen of the Fae. She also says that

Lizbet claimed your good buddy Queen Morgan had finally remerged and fully integrated with her, so no one needed to worry about her anymore. The thing that bothered Mrs. Moore the most was that she couldn't tell if it was real Lizbet or faux Lizbet."

"Poor Sheila, she's so been so jargogled since Fae Day. I'm glad she called you. Will you be able to tell the difference if it's my mistress just claiming to be Lizbet?"

"Yeah, definitely," Tanji said. "But if 'ol Queenie is trying to pretend that she's Lizbet instead of just sneaking around when Lizbet's out of it, that worries me. Do we let her think that she's fooled us, or do we confront her? I don't know what to do when I pick her up for school this morning if it's not Lizbet in the car with me."

"If, as you say, it's Morgan trying to convince you that she and Lizbet have finally remerged, let's go about this carefully. With Morgan in full control, she could take Lizbet away. I believe James, or more accurately, Myrddin, would be the only thing keeping her here, so we've got to keep quiet until we're sure we have a plan."

Morgan reluctantly dressed herself in Lizbet's ridiculous clothing but admired the way the style displayed the girl's athletic body to good effect. She tried to find suitable pieces in Lizbet's jewelry box, but none of the trinkets there were real gold and none contained precious stones. What status must this girl have if she owned nothing to flaunt her position?

She walked out the front door after hearing the signaling sound Tanji used to let Lizbet know she had arrived. She'd observed all of Lizbet's actions closely for over a month now, and she was sure that she could fool even Lizbet's best friend if she chose her actions carefully, sticking close to the behaviors and patterns of speech she had observed.

"Hey Tanj. Like the new me?" Morgan turned so that Tanji could see her smooth, wingless back as she approached the car.

"Whoa! When did that happen?"

"Morgan integrated yesterday, like, all of a sudden, after school. It was weird. But suddenly, I had all of her memories, and that was it. She was just in there. And I had the magic, so I made the wings go away."

"Seriously? I'm so happy for you, girl."

"Thanks. I've wanted it so badly. It's so hard to believe! I can get back to normal now. Although, of course, I had to hold court last night because Morgan is the fae's queen, and they really need her back to lead them. So, I've got to make sure that I'm doing my duty. It's going to be so hard to do when I'm stuck here so far away from most of the other fae."

"Court? What does that mean?"

"You know that half-fae have been showing up here because their communities don't accept them, and I need to be able to provide them with assistance of some kind. I've also been advised that the elves are unhappy about the number of half-fae that have been seeking them out; they want to be left alone. Some of the elven communities are even discussing arming themselves at their borders to keep the curious away. I need to help them understand that would be a bad idea. Morgan was a peacemaker. I need to be available to respond to all of my people so that things don't go wrong."

"Most of the elves are in France, Germany, and the UK,

right? I can't really see those modern democracies being okay with armed fae states inside their borders. So you can really help with that?"

"Of course. Even though I'm not present in Europe, Euphemia...," Morgan paused and corrected herself, "... Mona, who has discovered her dryad magic now, is lending me her talents to help me remain in communication with the fae court in Europe. I have Morgan's enormous body of wisdom in these things now, and I need to get involved again for the good of everyone."

Tanji wanted to roll her eyes at that, but instead she replied, "Yeah, I can see that. Good for you, girl."

Morgan exited the car after Tanji parked it in the parking lot of Lizbet's school and walked into the school next to Tanji, exactly as Lizbet did every day.

As they parted ways at the first hall, Tanji said, "Hey, good luck on that chemistry test today."

Morgan replied, "Thanks! Yeah, I guess I'll do okay."

Tanji turned right down the hall, out of sight of Lizbet. She grabbed her phone, pulled up the contact for Eamon, and hit the call button.

"Eamon? The chick I gave a ride to? Definitely not Lizbet...she almost has Lizbet down, but she's a real freaky version of her who doesn't think it's the least bit weird she's telling elves how to run their lives...yeah, no...she definitely has control of the magic because the wings are gone...it was like that was what she showed me to prove she was Lizbet and that instantly gives her cred. She hasn't got a clue what Lizbet is really about."

Tanji listened for a minute. "No...yeah...I'm sure. I

wished her good luck on a chemistry test and she didn't say a thing. She took chemistry last year. She's taking physics this year. Lizbet would have caught that mistake in a heartbeat...but I knew it wasn't her even before that. That was just to make sure my gut reaction was right."

Tanji stopped outside of her classroom. "Look, Eamon, I gotta go. Just catch up with me tonight, okay? We've got to do something about this."

Morgan congratulated herself on how well she'd managed Lizbet's school day. She was gracious when the human children noticed her lack of wings, and she felt sure that she'd behaved in every way as the girl Lizbet would in the same circumstances.

As she was walking down the hall, puffed up on her own self praise, a boy slapped her on the behind as he walked past, then continued quickly on, turning around once to wink.

Morgan raised her hand and the boy fell to the floor, gasping for air. She walked up to him and looked down as he continued to fight for breath, eyes desperate, begging her to stop. "No one touches the Queen of the Fae unless she wills it."

Morgan waved her hand, and the boy was able to breathe again. He was lucky. It was just in time.

"See that you stay very far away from me in the future."

"Moore!" a voice rang out behind her, as the boy scooted away from her across the floor, then stood up and hurried off.

Miss Armstrong stood in the middle of the hall, hands on her hips.

"Moore, we're going to the principal's office. Now."

Morgan had no intention of letting a human tell her what to do, but from previous encounters with this woman, she knew the woman had some kind of authority over the girl. She would need to comply if she meant to pass herself off as Lizbet. She fell into step behind the woman who stalked through the hall in front of her.

When Morgan spoke to the heavy set, bespectacled, middle-aged man whose nameplate identified him as Principal Stump, she made a point not to be too compliant. She thought the girl had more bearing than to allow herself to be manhandled. She advised him that no one should be allowed to touch her that way without her explicit permission. The principal agreed, but he also advised her that she knew that violent behavior was never tolerated on school grounds. The boy would be punished with an out-of-school suspension, but she would be placed in after-school detention for the day to think about how she could have handled the situation differently.

Morgan fumed on the inside but accepted detention without an argument.

CHAPTER NINETEEN
Stay With Me

TANJI SAT IN A lumpy, upholstered chair across from where James and Thomas filled the small couch in James's apartment.

"So...here's the thing...Lizbet's in detention for magically choking a boy who slapped her on the butt today. Which is too bad, because that kid needs to be choked once in a while, but that's also definitely not something Lizbet would do."

James nodded. "Yeah, I don't believe for a minute Lizbet would act like that, even if evil-Morgan integrated with her. I don't feel much influence from Myrddin's personality unless I'm actually seeking it out. It's been useful when I've had to deal with the elves, but I have to concentrate hard to get access to how to behave like Myrddin. Is that how it is with you and Langoureth?"

"Uhuh. Nail, meet head. I don't think it should be any different for Lizbet and Morgan. Morgan finally figured something out that let her get her way."

"Can you think of anything that Lizbet has been doing differently in the past few days?"

"She was trying to stay awake so that Morgan couldn't take her over again. She was *really* upset about Morgan coming on to you. Pretty much, it was, 'no way is that witch stealing my boyfriend!'." Tanji glanced to Thomas. "Thomas and I worked up a potion that helped her stay awake and she was taking that, but it only lasted a few hours at a time. She also tried to make sure that someone was with her when she was sleeping, like when you were there the day she had to come home from school."

"Yeah, but that didn't work, because that's the day Morgan got friendly with me. Was Lizbet taking the potion then?"

"No. We hadn't made it yet."

"Thomas, what potion did you make her? I don't remember telling you about any potions that would help someone stay awake."

Thomas shook his head, "No, it wasn't one you gave me. Lizbet gave me the potion. She'd written it down in the old druid hand and gave it to me to make for her. But I couldn't read it, so I asked Tanji to help. I assumed she got it from the human Morgan's memories."

"That just doesn't sound right—Thomas, when did she give it to you?" James asked.

"The other day, right after you called the lightning."

James and Tanji exchanged glances. "Oh great..." said James. "Okay, kids. First, Thomas—I'll need to know everything that was in that potion. Second, Tanji—go home, get Langoureth's book, and come right back. We may need it."

Bobby went out to the backyard after school and was surprised to find that the gnomes were arrayed in a circle, looking solemn rather than playing.

Gurrdenn, who wore the hollowed out head of a rat as a headpiece, walked out from the center of the circle and took his hand, pulling him to the center to sit on the small pile of furs where Gurrdenn had previously been sitting. One of the furs looked suspiciously like a stray cat that had been roaming the neighborhood last week. Bobby sat down, expecting whatever the gnomes were doing to soon turn into a game, but instead, the gnomes stood up and began to walk solemnly in a circle, chanting quietly.

Bobby knew what would happen—in a minute, they would start to act silly and noisy again, and, of course, they did. And then he expected them to break out dancing, and, of course, they did. He figured it was time for him to stand up and join in, and, of course, he did, starting out by spinning around and laughing loudly in the center of the circle.

It was only when he tried to leave the center and join the circle that he realized something was wrong.

Bobby ran into an invisible wall after walking three feet or so, just inside where the gnomes circled around him. He tried to move out into the circle on another side, and he was trapped there, too.

He put his hands up in front of him and felt along the invisible barrier. It went all the way around him, following the gnome's circle exactly. He was trapped. He didn't know what to think.

"Gurrdenn?"

"Bobby", the gnome answered back.

"What kind of game is this?"

"Bobby stay. Bobby no school. No father take away. Bobby stay."

Bobby looked down at him, wide-eyed, then he shouted as loud as he could, "Mom! Mom! Help, mom!"

His mother poked her head out into the back yard and said, "Bobby, what's wrong?"

"Mom, can you come out? Please. I...the gnomes..."

Bobby could see that mom look worried. She walked quickly out to the garden and straight to her son. Bobby thought she'd run into the invisible wall, but she walked right up to him and kneeled down. "What's wrong, sweetie?"

Bobby felt stupid for letting the gnomes trick him with one of their games. He reached out and took her hand and said, "Nothing, mom. I just wanted to know if you would color with me. Let's go in the house."

"Sure, I've got a little while before I need to start getting dinner ready. Maybe you can even help me with that."

It all would have been fine if his mom hadn't walked through the invisible wall without him.

Mom turned back to look at him as his hand pulled out of hers. From knee level, a small voice piped up to him, "Bobby stay."

James kept his voice down as he talked into the phone, "Eamon, we've got unintended consequences in spades... you better get over here to the Moores'."

James turned around and walked back to where Sheila Moore sat on the ground with her arm around her son, who lay his head on her shoulder and looked ready to burst into tears.

James crouched down so that he was near eye level with the boy, "Hey, buddy, no problem. Eamon's on his way over, and between the two of us, we'll take care of it. If the world's most powerful wizard and a short guy with the world's ugliest hair can't sort this out..."

He'd hoped Bobby might laugh at that. He didn't.

The gnomes had gone about their business for the most part now that their god wouldn't be taking off anytime soon. The majority of the huddle was trying to scare up a bird or two for dinner in the ferns at the back of the yard, but James could see Gurrdenn lurking behind the birdbath, keeping an eye on Bobby and Sheila.

James stood up and walked toward him, "Gurrdenn, come on out here for a minute."

The gnome walked forward and stood looking up at James.

"Let Bobby go. He won't leave you, but he needs to be freed."

"No."

"Be reasonable. Bobby's just a little boy."

"No."

"Sheesh. Well, thanks for that productive talk."

From behind, James heard, "Dinnae I tell ye not to try to reason with a gnome? Stubbornest creatures alive. Mostly, they just don't have enough room in their tiny brains to reverse a decision. No, we'll need something more powerful. Something a bit dangerous perhaps."

Eamon walked forward and stood half a foot away from the gnome, looking down at him. They stood and stared at each for a moment, neither one looking away despite the intensity of their stares. Then Eamon spoke, "D'ye know, I'm thinking that we could have Lizbet ask her pet elf to bring one of those dragons over from Europe. Gurrdenn, you've heard the tales, haven't ye? Isn't that why the gnomes ended up crossing the seas on the ships anyway, to escape them? To be able to go above the ground again without fear of being dinner?"

Gurrdenn didn't flinch. "Bobby stay."

"Right, like I said...stubborn. Join me on the patio, lad?" he said, catching James's eye and inclining his head toward the house. "We'll need to think on this at greater length."

Eamon then moved his attention to Bobby's mother. Moore, "Sheila, could you join us for a moment? I have a request."

When Sheila left Bobby and joined them, Eamon asked her to try to keep Lizbet away from the house for a while. Morgan would be of no use, and having her there might make the situation worse, as Morgan truly hated gnomes. Sheila went into the house to make the call.

"Sure, Mrs. M, I can do that. Good luck...I'm sure that it won't go on for much longer...I'm sure James can help... and I can handle the Queen. She thinks I've been taken in, so it's no biggie to keep up the charade."

Tanji grabbed her car keys out of her purse, picked up her phone, and typed a text to Lizbet as she waved to Thomas on her way out of the apartment:

"pk u up at skl and eat at mine 2nite - parents sd yes"

Tanji waited for a response. It came back quickly.

"ok I will be out front"

Tanji slid into the driver's seat of the car and turned the music on loud. She wasn't looking forward to pretending she was enjoying Morgan's company.

~~*

Morgan waved her hand in front of Mr. Hill's face and he started moving again. She tried so very hard not to throw her head back and laugh as she said, "Five o'clock, Mr. Hill. Time for us to go." The teacher looked at the clock, disoriented.

The other kids, who'd stayed playing cards and having a fine time directly underneath the nose of the frozen teacher, snickered as they followed her out.

CHAPTER TWENTY
Mama Come Get Your Baby Boy

SHEILA AND BOBBY PUT up the pup tent, and Sheila handed the sleeping bags in to her son. If he was trapped, she could at least try to make it seem fun while they waited for a solution.

"You know what? What we need to really make this fun is some snacks...I have just the thing. I'll be right back."

Sheila went to the house and returned with a bag of snack-size chocolate bars she kept for Bobby's daily lunch-bag treat. She handed one to him and peeled the wrapper off her own. Then, she opened her laptop and accessed the family's streaming movie account and started up Bobby's favorite movie.

"Thanks, mom!"

"It's a special occasion, isn't it? How often do you get to camp out on a school night, right?" Sheila said to the now contented-looking boy. She looked up to where James and

Eamon were talking animatedly on the porch. "Honey, I'm going to talk to James for a minute, and then I'll be back to watch the movie with you."

Sheila walked up to the porch and sat on the far side of the table between James and Eamon so that she could keep an eye on Bobby in the garden, not that he was going anywhere any time soon.

She listened for a while as the other two talked about possible solutions to the problem but broke in when Eamon said, "Well, if the gnomes that cast the spell die, then the spell is released..."

"You're going to kill the gnomes? I don't think so!"

"Sheila, I'm sorry. I wasn't suggestin' that we do away with them necessarily. I'm just layin' out all the options... the thing is, and I hate to say it, but James and I might have precipitated this problem. We were tryin' to prevent the gnomes following Bobby to school, as they seem to be very protective of him these days. There was a second scuffle with another child, one of Bobby's friends..."

"I didn't know about that."

"No, the child wasn't badly hurt, and the school didn't know that the gnomes were involved...but it was gettin' out of hand, so we tricked one of the gnomes into putting up a barrier so that they can't leave the yard. We thought that would take care of things, but as ye see, now they won't let Bobby leave, either."

"Well, I might have had a part in that, too. Bobby's father came by last night, threatening to take him back to his place. I stopped that cold, but Gurrdenn's always looking in at the windows for Bobby—it's been creepy lately, really. He might have heard us talking...it got...heated."

"Aye, that makes sense. If they feared he'd be taken

away, that might cause them to restrict the lad's range of movement."

"Eamon, I don't care *why* they did it. And all of us did what we thought was going to be best for Bobby, so let's just find a way to solve the problem and not worry about who to blame."

"Sheila, we've not hit on a solution yet. I'll talk to their elders, and perhaps we can strike a deal with them in time, but it's difficult to reason with a gnome. If they believe somethin', it's nearly impossible to get them to listen to the other side."

"Ah, like children, then."

"As you say. Perhaps you should take a run at them. You've more experience in that area than either James or I do."

"If you don't have any success, I certainly will."

"And then, after we've rescued this one, we need to rescue your other child who's trapped in a very different way. I'm so sorry, Sheila, for everything that's happened."

Tanji walked into the den, dropped the box of twigs, herbs, and colored twine they would use to make the pixie wards on the coffee table, and sat down on the couch next to pretend-Lizbet.

"Any ideas for a movie while we knock out pixie wards?"

Lizbet shook her head, "You go ahead and choose."

Tanji checked her streaming movie queue and settled on a superhero flick, something escapist that didn't have magic in it. Once upon a time she enjoyed fantasy movies, but now that she understood magic and magical creatures, they seemed silly. Magic was both more and less than the way it was portrayed. Now that the fae had returned, the whole genre was going to need a makeover—and it certainly couldn't be called "fantasy" anymore.

She brought microwave popcorn and iced tea out to the table, and they worked silently while they watched the movie. Tanji tried to get some social going, but every time she did, "Lizbet" would reply with only "yes" or "no" or just nod. Dull. She wanted her friend back.

Whatever. Decent movie. Salty popcorn. The Queen wasn't getting Lizbet into any trouble at the moment, and they were getting a lot of pixie wards done for the store, and that store was going to pay for her trip to Scotland to see Langoureth's country for herself. She tried hard to ignore the fact that her best friend was in serious danger and focus on other things. At least 'ol Queenie wasn't flying Lizbet's body around a couple of countries for her own nefarious purposes tonight.

Tanji's phone rang. When she looked at the caller information, she excused herself and went to her room to take the call.

"Yeah, I can get her back there. I think she's bored out of her mind anyway...okay, I'll try. See ya."

CHAPTER TWENTY-ONE

Rescue Me

TANJI PULLED HER CAR into the driveway behind Mrs. Moore's SUV. She watched Lizbet step out of the car regally—she had to admit that Morgan certainly had the bearing of a queen. She knew how to make everything look graceful and controlled. So completely not like her charge-right-into-the-situation and trip-on-the-way-in best friend.

The girls walked toward the front door, but they turned when a voice behind them called out, "Your majesty, I seek an audience. I've had communication from the elders." The speaker was Freoric.

Lizbet turned to Tanji and said, "Why don't you go ahead and go in. I'll just be a minute. Grab my blue pajamas. You know where they are."

"Sure, not a problem," Tanji said, as she continued to the front door and let herself in.

She hurried through the house and into the backyard. Everything looked pretty normal, except for the worried looks on the faces of human and fae alike.

She approached James and Eamon where they stood on the porch watching Sheila entertaining her son just in front of a small pup tent.

"She stopped outside to talk to Freoric. That elf gives me the willies. She'll probably be heading into the house soon," Tanji said to James.

"Okay then, it might work out better if I try to head her off," said James, "Let's just hope she's as into me as I think she is, or this is never going to work."

～～*

As James opened the front door and stepped out onto the walk, he wondered if he had the guts to pull it off. He had to convince Morgan that he thought she was Lizbet and that he couldn't keep his hands off of her for another minute. It would take everything he had to betray Lizbet that way. He was tempted to try to call on some of Myrddin's magic instead, but there was a chance he would fail against someone as powerful as Morgan. It would also completely blow his cover. His only option was to play her and hope it worked.

"Lizbet?" he called out to the woman who was still engaged in an animated conversation with the elf.

She turned quickly at the sound of his voice. "Myrddin. What are you doing here? I wasn't expecting you."

James pretended not to notice she'd called him Myrddin. "I couldn't stop thinking about you, and I realized that I just had to see you. I was disappointed when your mother told me you weren't home, but when I found out Bobby may be in danger, I stayed to help."

"You couldn't stop thinking about me?"

As soon as she asked that question, James feared there was nothing of Lizbet still there within her body. Lizbet's only and immediate concern would have been Bobby, not her relationship with James. James steeled himself, walked to her, and took her hand. "You're all I ever think about."

Lizbet turned to the elf and said, "Freoric, we'll speak later. I've no need for you at the moment."

Freoric's eyes hardened, but he went to one knee and bowed his head, then stood, turned, and walked to a discreet distance at the side of the yard, continuing to stand guard. He kept his eyes to the street.

Satisfied that they now had their privacy, Morgan put her arms around James's neck and pulled him close. They kissed for a long time. James tried hard to forget he was kissing the woman who had replaced the girl he cared so much about. From Morgan's side, the kiss was passionate, from James's it was merely compliant, going through the motions.

Morgan pulled away from him, "What's wrong? I could feel you pulling away."

"Lizbet, I... I'm worried about Bobby. The gnomes have him trapped."

"Those ridiculous gnomes! I cannot bear gnomes. I should have gotten rid of them when I had the chance."

"I know, but Bobby really likes them, and now it's... they've used their magic to prevent him from leaving the yard. Eamon is trying to talk them into releasing him, but he's not having any luck so far. I think it's going to take someone with a lot more presence than a gruagach to handle the situation. I would be a lot less distracted if I knew Bobby was safe. I'm sure you would be, too."

Morgan responded teasingly, and she stroked her hand

across his chest as she spoke, "If it would make you kiss me with passion, James, I'm sure I have the presence to handle that situation."

James watched Morgan's face change, quickly moving to an expression of false concern. She continued, "Yes, I love Bobby so much. I'm sure that I can help."

He turned toward the door then, still holding her hand to lead her. "I'm so glad you can help! We'll have more time together after this situation is fixed up. Staying away from you has been torture."

On the inside, James cringed with every word. He was more than grateful that mind reading was not a fae talent.

Morgan exited the house onto the patio, still holding James's hand. She looked into the back yard where Bobby and his mother were watching a video. Tanji was sitting in one of the patio chairs and did not appear to have collected Lizbet's bedclothes as instructed. Eamon came to her, went to one knee, and bowed his head.

"You may rise."

"Thank ye, mistress. Has James told you what happened?"

"He's told me that Bobby is trapped by the gnomes."

"Aye, they've used their magic to stick him in place with a barrier that only allows objects that are not Bobby to pass through. We can pass through and visit, but Bobby can't come out. As you can imagine, the boy's terrified. Your mother's got him calmed a bit now, but she can't live in the back yard forever. Neither of them can."

"Let me think for a minute how I could take him through the barrier. Certainly, I can break the magic of a huddle of gnomes."

"Aye, mistress, I know you can. We're all countin' on it."

She squeezed James's hand, "I have it. It's simple."

Morgan walked toward the tent purposefully. As she did, she saw several gnomes run quickly to their burrow holes, shouting a warning to others, "the queen, the queen!" and then disappear inside. Once she'd freed Bobby to please James, she'd take care of the gnomes permanently. If she had to live, even for a brief time, in this residence, she would no longer permit a gnome-infested garden.

When Morgan was in front of Bobby, she offered him her hand, "Bobby, take my hand. We're walking out of here."

Bobby took her hand and stood up. Morgan saw Sheila watching her closely, her expression guarded. She spoke as she hoped the girl would speak to her mother, "It's okay, mom. Bobby's safe with me. He always is."

Then, she walked toward the barrier with Bobby's hand in hers, secure in the knowledge that the ward she placed around him with her quiet chanting would prevent any magic from acting on him as long as she held his hand.

Eamon hoped that Lizbet was conscious enough inside her mind to realize what was happening. They'd laid all of their bets on Lizbet being strong enough to save herself from the queen if they provided the right kind of help.

He'd known it wouldn't be a pleasant thing to watch, but he couldn't take his eyes off of the barrier for long. He glanced quickly at Sheila and then at James. Each of them was riveted in place, barely breathing. His eyes moved back to where Bobby held his sister's hand and walked forward.

It began.

Bobby went straight through and turned to tug on

Lizbet's hand with both of his as she hit the barrier. A look of struggle, pain, and surprise appeared on her face as the boundary of her body blurred where it met the magical fence.

Almost as quickly, her face contorted with rage and she began to backup, pulling Bobby with her. "You think you've fooled me?" she screamed. "Will you really give up the life of this child to capture me?"

Eamon looked at Sheila, who gasped, fear darkening her face. They hadn't thought of the danger to the boy. No one could imagine Lizbet harming him.

Nor could Lizbet. With that threat, she woke up and fought for control, her face a mask of determination, her hand in Bobby's. "Pull harder," she urged him through gritted teeth. "It's working!"

The confused form that was now half young girl and half elderly fae started to push through, both of them screaming as their essences and bodies were ripped apart.

Eamon, because of his furious speed, was the first to reach her. He grabbed her other hand as Lizbet strained to shed the queen's body. Only a heartbeat later, James replaced Bobby and all three of them shouted encouragement to her as they helped her struggle away from the fae who had inhabited her.

They tugged and tugged for only a matter of minutes, but to all of them, it felt like hours.

When Lizbet pulled the last of her body through, she collapsed on the outside of the barrier, rocking and moaning, her arms wrapped around her body as the pain of the separation still clung to her.

Morgan fell to the ground behind her.

Sheila rushed forward with Bobby's sleeping bag to cover the elderly fae's nakedness. The gnomes had done their job perfectly. They'd changed the barrier to prevent only things that were part of Morgan from leaving.

After Sheila covered Morgan, she moved quickly outside of the barrier to go to her daughter who was now safe in James's arms. She touched Lizbet's cheek and asked, "How are you? Are you okay?"

Lizbet smiled weakly at the friends and family whose faces, stiff with concern, surrounded her. She grimaced. "Really? That was the best plan you could come up with?"

James laughed. His Lizbet was back. Soon Sheila, Tanji, and Bobby joined in, everyone engaging in an awkward but effective group hug, expressions changing from concern to relief.

Once he saw that Lizbet was safe, Eamon went to the queen he had served for so many, many years and cushioned her head on his lap, smoothing her hair. Her face was pale and feverish, her body stiffened by pain.

"Eamon, what have you done? I..."

"Mistress, I'm sorry. The gnomes let the magic pass through with Lizbet. Without the magic, I fear the same disease that killed the human side of you will now run its course. I think you've very little time."

"I don't want to die, Eamon."

"I know. I'd hoped the disease had left you long ago, but we didn't have any choice that we knew for sure would save you. We couldn't leave the magic with you; it would be far too dangerous. It wasn't right what you did, to try to take over a life that didn't belong to you. You should have been content to share a part of what Lizbet and James will have together rather than try to bring Myrddin back to you."

"But the fae...they'll split apart without me to guide them, do you care nothing for them? The elves will go on the hunt for the gruagach again, as they did until I intervened all those years ago."

"Perhaps they will mistress. I have no way of knowing. I do know that once she becomes accustomed to the idea, Lizbet will make a kind and strong queen, just as you were a thousand years ago, before your sorrow destroyed you."

Eamon stayed with his mistress, holding her hand. It wasn't long until she relaxed, and her spirit returned to the aether.

CHAPTER TWENTY-TWO
Bury Your Dead

WHEN LIZBET MATERIALIZED UP the hill from the McShane farm, she felt a brief twinge of nostalgia. Back when she was just a regular girl, she'd depended on a bike to get her to this spot rather than riding the aether from Ohio to Scotland in moments. No going back, though. Being queen was the new normal, and she was learning to deal with it.

On the way down to the farm, she hoped the kind, elderly woman who had helped her only two months ago would be receptive to her request.

Lizbet knocked on the door tentatively and smiled when Mrs. McShane answered, "Hi...do you remember me from when I was here before?"

"I do, lass. But I remember you better for freeing the fae. Who would have thought it? My father would have roared with joy. He was always a believer." Mrs. McShane stepped back from the door and beckoned her foward. "Come inside then. I'll get the tea, shall I?"

Once Mrs. McShane had Lizbet seated comfortably on the couch with a cup of tea for one hand and a sweet biscuit for the other, she said, "Now, lassie. To what do I owe this visit from a queen?"

"Do you remember that we were looking for a grave when we were here before?"

"Aye, I do. And that you found what you were looking for."

"So, you were the one who told us that the Victorians called that grave the 'fairy grave', and they were pretty close to right. A powerful sorcerer who was half-fae was buried there. His name was Myrddin, but you would probably know him as Merlin."

"Och, now ye're just pulling me leg, lassie."

"No, it was Myrddin. He's James's half-fae, as it turns out, just as Morgan Le Fae was mine."

"It's an interesting history lesson, but I think you're not here to educate me on the history of the fae. You might as well come out with it."

"No, I'm not here for a history lesson, that's for sure. I'm here to ask you a favor, but I wanted to put some things in context for you, so that you would understand why."

"Might as well just say it, lassie, I'm not getting any younger while I wait."

"Yesterday, Morgan Le Fae passed away—we were separated from each other physically, and when we were, she didn't survive it. I and some of my friends would like to bring her back here to be with Myrddin who was the only love of her hundreds of years of life. We want to show our respects to her in the best way we can."

"That's quite a request, lass, but I'll honor my own

father by telling you yes. He'd be well pleased to know that not just one but two fae are resting comfortably up there on the hill."

Lizbet went to the old woman and hugged her gently. "Thank you. It would have meant everything to her."

"How could a good Scots woman deny a request from the faery queen?"

"Thank you, Thomas, for helping me with this. I don't have the first idea how to go about dressing Morgan's body for burial," Eamon said as Thomas wrapped Morgan's body in linens soaked in herbs and fine mud, then ran his hands over the wraps to smooth it to her cold skin. "Gruagachs serve in many ways, but our bond is severed at death. No gruagach likes a graveyard.

"I consider it an honor." Thomas soaked another piece of cloth and repeated the operation. "She was Queen of the Fae. She was my mistress, too. How could I refuse her?"

CHAPTER TWENTY-THREE
First Date

J AMES SAT ON THE edge of the his bed as Thomas made a final clothing check in the mirror on the back of the bedroom door. The air was thick with the scent of lavender and mint his roommate had been simmering all day to try to keep his anxiety in check.

"Tom, I feel like a proud parent sending you out on your first date tonight. Are you sure you don't want Lizbet and me to come along and keep you from making a complete fool of yourself?"

"Thanks, but I'd rather make a git of myself with as few people present as possible, if it's fine with you." Thomas gave a final glance at himself in the mirror on the back of the bedroom door and pushed back a curl that had fallen over his eye. "Anyway, her father's going to be joining us, so no pressure there."

James smiled and then leaned forward with a more

serious expression, "I'm happy for you. I can tell you're uncomfortable with this, but I think Tanji gets that. She may seem pushy, but that's just surface. She knows you've spent six lifetimes as a monk. I'm sure she won't try to rush things."

"Maybe if I'd known her before this—in a lifetime when she wasn't my great-aunt, I mean—I wouldn't have been such a successful monk." Thomas kept a straight face as he said it, then turned to James and burst into a grin, raising his hand, palm out, "High five, mate! I've got a date!"

* ～ * ～ *

Tanji ran past her father as he walked to answer the door when the doorbell rang. "I've got it, dad! It's Thomas. He's coming to dinner, remember?"

Ron turned and walked back to the den to finish his show, shaking his head and rolling his eyes. Like he could forget! He never would have believed his daughter could fall for the monkish type, but she'd begged for her father to allow a trial date and approve of Thomas despite the difference in their ages. When you have a force of nature for a daughter, it's nearly impossible to resist her.

EPILOGUE
Season Of The Fall

THE FIRST SNOW STARTED to fall that year as Tanji twirled in the red satin dress and the dress's full skirts flew out around her. She admired the effect in Lizbet's full-length mirror.

"Morgan was a definite pain, but she had some fine taste in gowns. I can seriously have this for homecoming? My dad gave me $150 to spend and I've got my earnings from my first week in the shop, but with this dress? That can go into my Scottish vacation fund instead. But girl, you should have aethered me there for the funeral, and I could have visited a lot sooner."

"Yeah, yeah. There you go again with 'why did you leave me behind?' It's been almost a month. Time to drop it," Lizbet said, "Eamon wanted it to be small and quiet, I've told you that. It was somber, Tanj. I mean, really somber.

Eamon and James aren't proud of what they had to do to save me, and I'm not real cool with my part in it, either."

Tanji's look went serious. "Yeah, I didn't mean to be flip. I'm sorry."

"Like you can be serious in satin," Lizbet laughed and ran her hands down the sides of the blue velvet gown she was wearing, "This one isn't bad when you get used to how fancy it is. You know what it needs?"

"It looks great with just your amulet."

"You think too small, Tanj. I mean, if James and I and you and Thomas are going to really make a splash..." Lizbet concentrated and winced a little as she felt the tearing feeling around her shoulder blades that she now accepted as her price to pay for controlling Morgan's magic. If things were never really going to be normal again: might as well embrace the things she had. *Welcome to the new normal, Lizbet,* she thought as she spread the wings that coordinated so well with the royal blue of the dress. "Every once in a while, girl, I need to work the wings because the wings are *fierce.*"

~~*

Mona slipped out of her shoes and dug her toes into the frozen mulch beneath the dusting of snow, barely noticing the cold. As she did, roots reached out from her feet into the earth and her body stiffened, her trunk lengthening and branches growing up toward the sky. The transformation was painless now—could always have been, if Morgan had told her about the potion that would allow her human cells to transform without the agony. But Morgan hadn't cared. She'd used Mona and let her suffer.

The voices began to fill her. She searched for the one

voice she wished to communicate with that day: the voice of her sister fae, a full dryad named Eugenia who helped Mona keep Lizbet informed about what was happening among the fae in Europe. She did this gladly—Sheila was a good friend, and her daughter was turning into a good queen, traveling regularly between Ohio and Scotland on the aether while still managing to keep up with her schoolwork. Lizbet was concerned about the elves and wanted to know all the rumors as soon as they occurred.

Mona listened silently to Eugenia's urgent whisperings, anxiety growing within her as she continued to transform. If what Eugenia was passing along was true, humans were now in grave danger from the elves.

Even more, her own queen was under threat from an evil here at home. She must collect the information quickly instead of lingering in the joys of nature and sharing gossip with her sister dryad. She needed to inform her queen.

She was more tree than human by then, beginning to turn from hearing sound to sensing vibrations through leaves and bark and small twigs. But even then, she heard the laughter. Deep, masculine laughter.

Her essence had not fully hardened into the protective strength of the tree when the arrow flew from the bushes and struck through her very human heart.

The wood and sap hardened around it. The fletched end stuck out from the bark to mark where it had found its target.

She knew she could not return to her human form or she would die from the wound. Staying here in this peaceful place would not be so bad. Her human memories would eventually fade and she would become one with the woods, a part of nature.

But who would warn the queen if she could not?

ABOUT THE AUTHOR

Jill Nojack is a writer, musician and artist. She has published several short works (stories and poetry) in small press. Her first published novel, Magic Unbound, Book One in the Fae Unbound Series, was released in November, 2013. There are now four books in the series.

When she isn't exploring her creative side, Jill enjoys laughing too loud and long in public, long bike rides, and talking about herself in third person. She resides in the great American Midwest with a long-suffering cat and makes her living as a computer tech, because, if you're lucky, that's what you do with degrees in English and Sociology.

Visit www.faeunbound.com for more information about the series along with related special content. You can sign up for the newsletter if you would like to be notified of new releases.